PEANUT BUTTER AND JELLY

BEN CLANTON

tundra

FOR ALEX COX!
KEEP SPREADING THE AWESOMENESS!

Text and illustrations copyright © 2018 by Ben Clanton

Tundra Books, an imprint of Penguin Random House Canada Young Readers, a Penguin Random House Company

Library and Archives Canada Cataloguing in Publication

Clanton, Ben, 1988-, author, illustrator
Peanut butter and Jelly / Ben Clanton.

(A Narwhal and Jelly book)
Issued in print and electronic formats.
ISBN 978-0-7352-6245-4 (hardcover).–ISBN 978-0-7352-6246-1 (softcover)
ISBN 978-0-7352-6247-8 (epub)

I. Title. II. Series: Clanton, Ben, 1988- . Narwhal and Jelly book

PZ7.C523Pea 2019   j813'.6   C2018-901240-4

Published simultaneously in the United States of America by Tundra Books of Northern New York, an imprint of Penguin Random House Canada Young Readers, a Penguin Random House Company

Library of Congress Control Number: 2017939300

Edited by Tara Walker and Jessica Burgess
Designed by Ben Clanton and Andrew Roberts
The artwork in this book was rendered in colored pencil, watercolor and ink, and colored digitally.
The text was handlettered by Ben Clanton.

Photos: (waffle) © Tiger Images/Shutterstock; (strawberry) © Valentina Razumova/Shutterstock; (pickle) © dominitsky/Shutterstock; (boom box) © valio84sl/Thinkstock; (jars) © choness/Thinkstock; (peanuts) © Zoonar/homydesign/Thinkstock; (jam on bread) © George Doyle/Thinkstock; (peanut butter toast) © NicholasBPhotography/Thinkstock

Printed and bound in China

www.penguinrandomhouse.ca

This edition for the Narwhal and Jelly Box Set, ISBN 978-0-7352-6591-2

4 5   23 22 21

CONTENTS

5 A SWEET AND SALTY STORY!

31 DELICIOUS FACTS

33 AHOY, PEANUT BUTTER?

45 SUPER WAFFLE AND STRAWBERRY SIDEKICK VS. PB&J

49 PEANUT A.K.A. mini NARWHAL

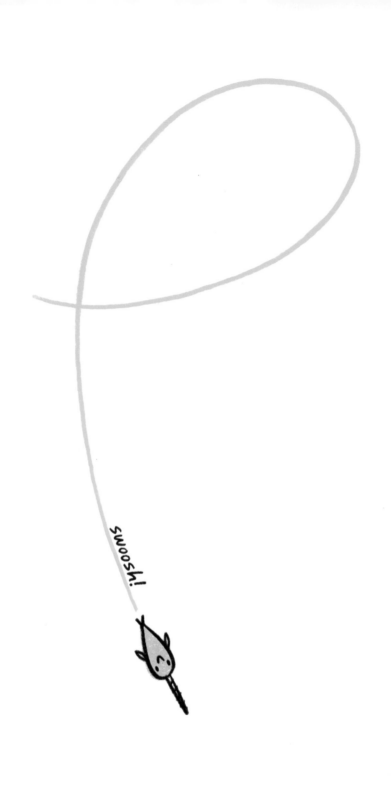

swoosh!

A SWEET AND SALTY STORY!

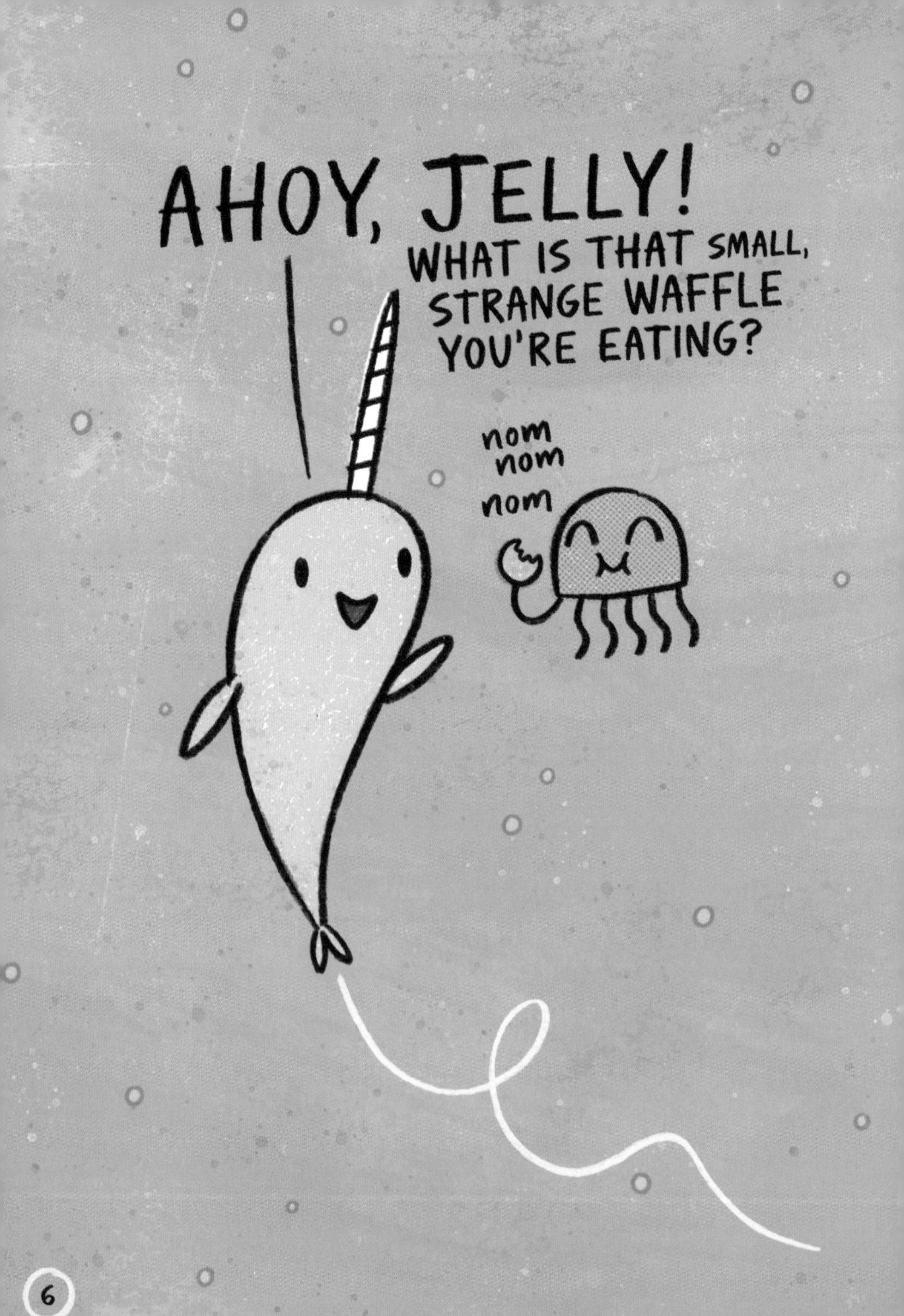
AHOY, JELLY!
WHAT IS THAT SMALL, STRANGE WAFFLE YOU'RE EATING?
nom nom nom

UM...NARWHAL,
THIS IS **NOT** A WAFFLE.
IT IS A PEANUT BUTTER
COOKIE.

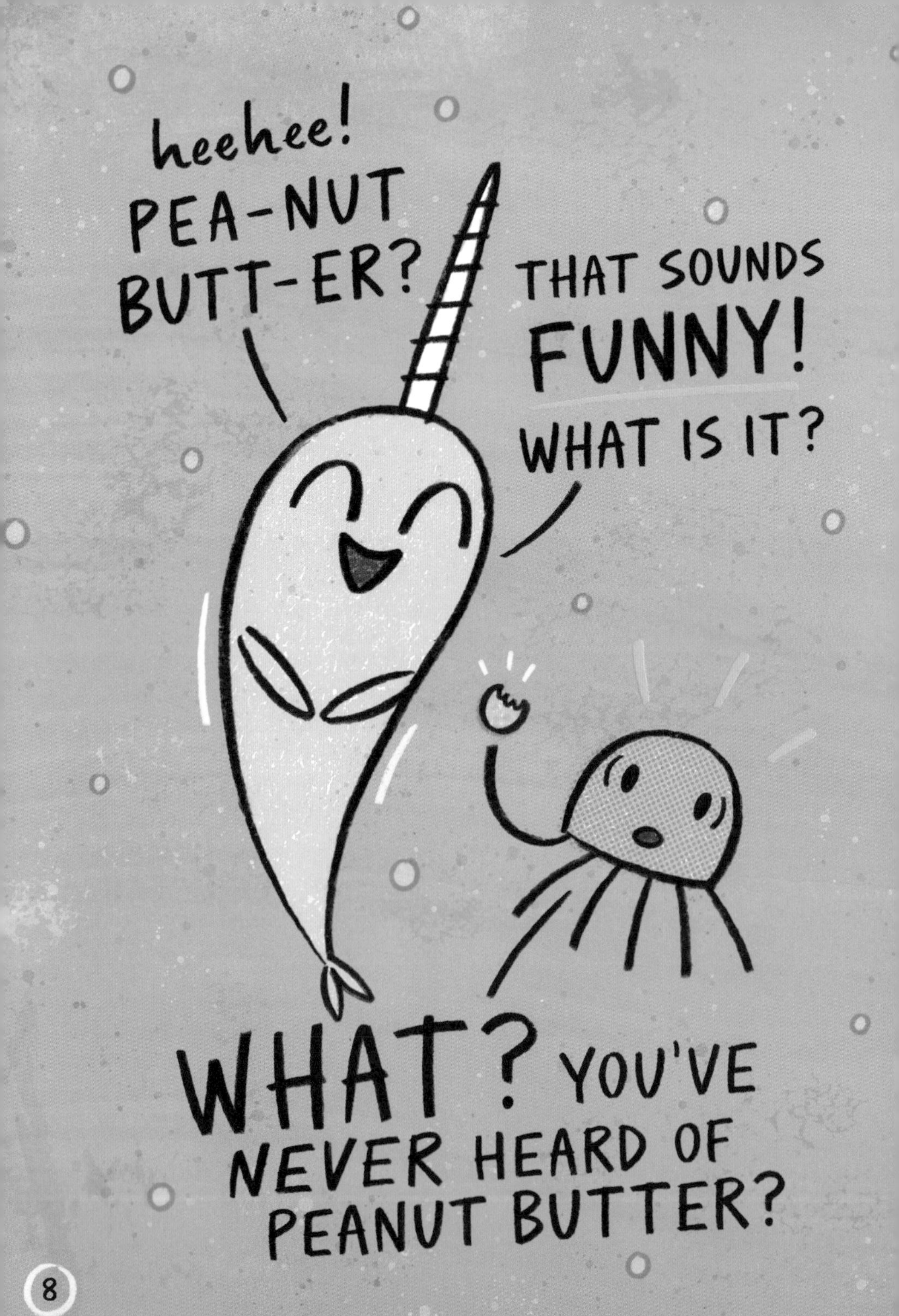
heehee! PEA-NUT BUTT-ER?
THAT SOUNDS FUNNY! WHAT IS IT?
WHAT? YOU'VE NEVER HEARD OF PEANUT BUTTER?

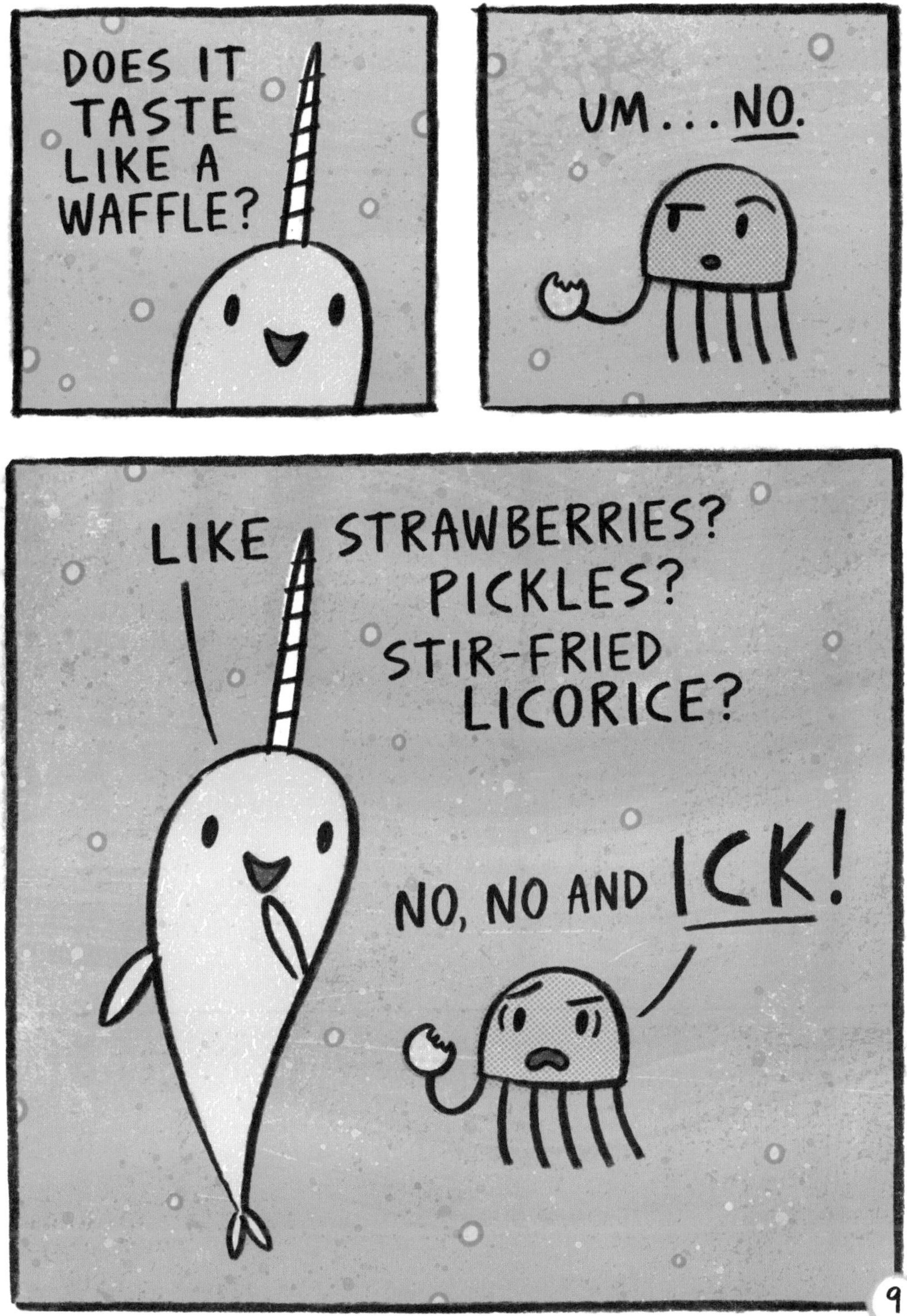
DOES IT TASTE LIKE A WAFFLE?
UM... NO.
LIKE STRAWBERRIES? PICKLES? STIR-FRIED LICORICE?
NO, NO AND ICK!

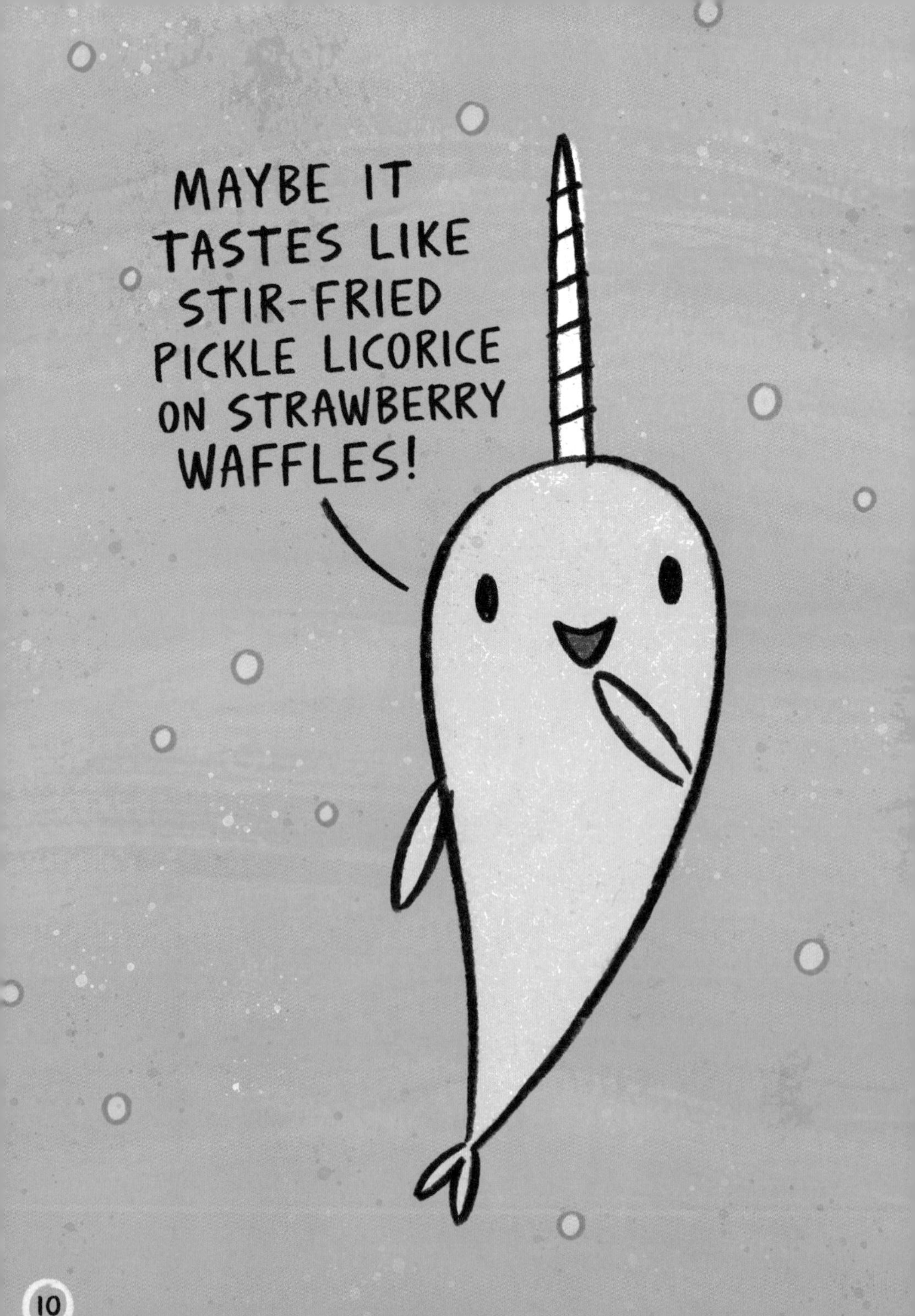
MAYBE IT TASTES LIKE STIR-FRIED PICKLE LICORICE ON STRAWBERRY WAFFLES!

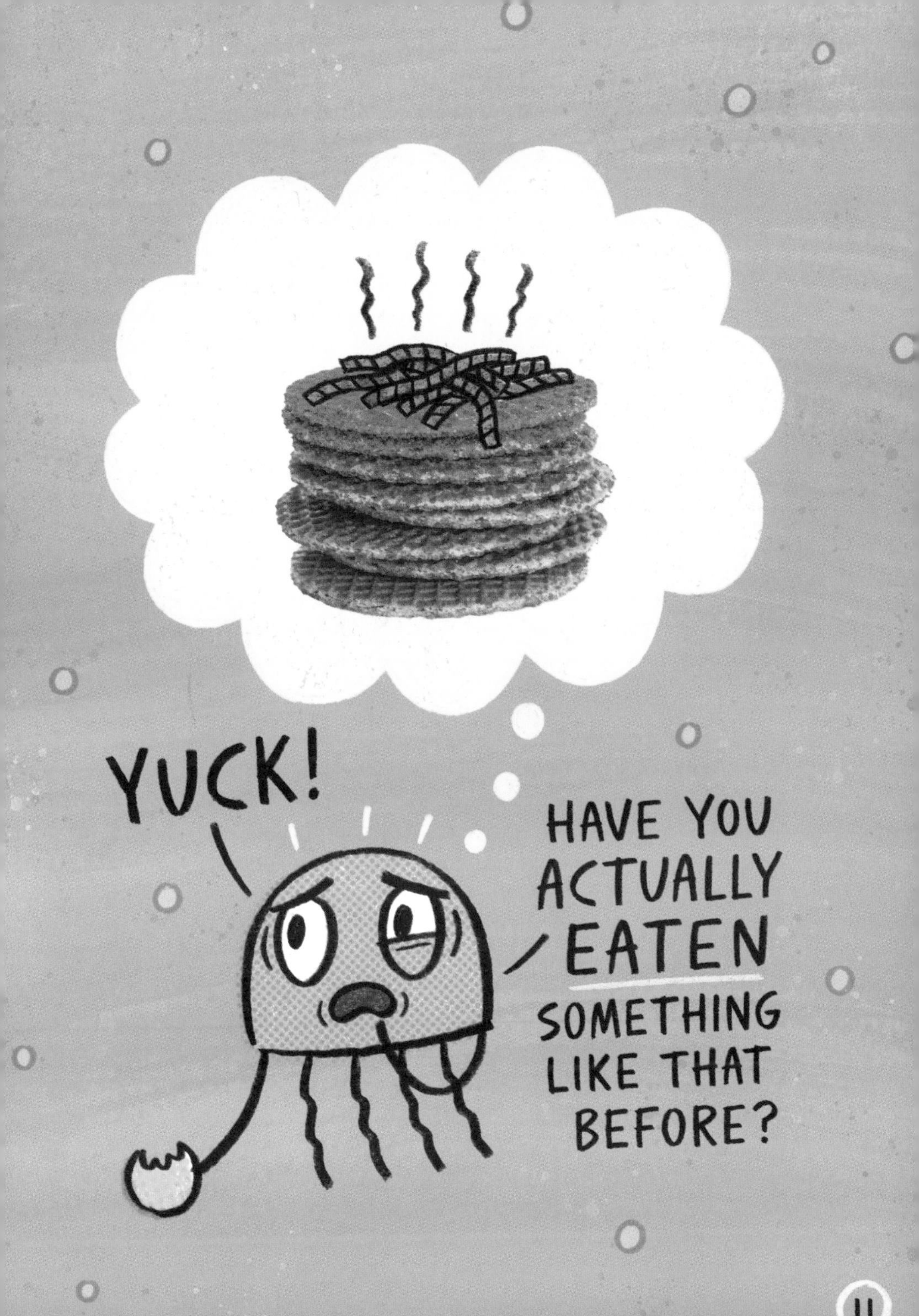
YUCK!
HAVE YOU ACTUALLY EATEN SOMETHING LIKE THAT BEFORE?

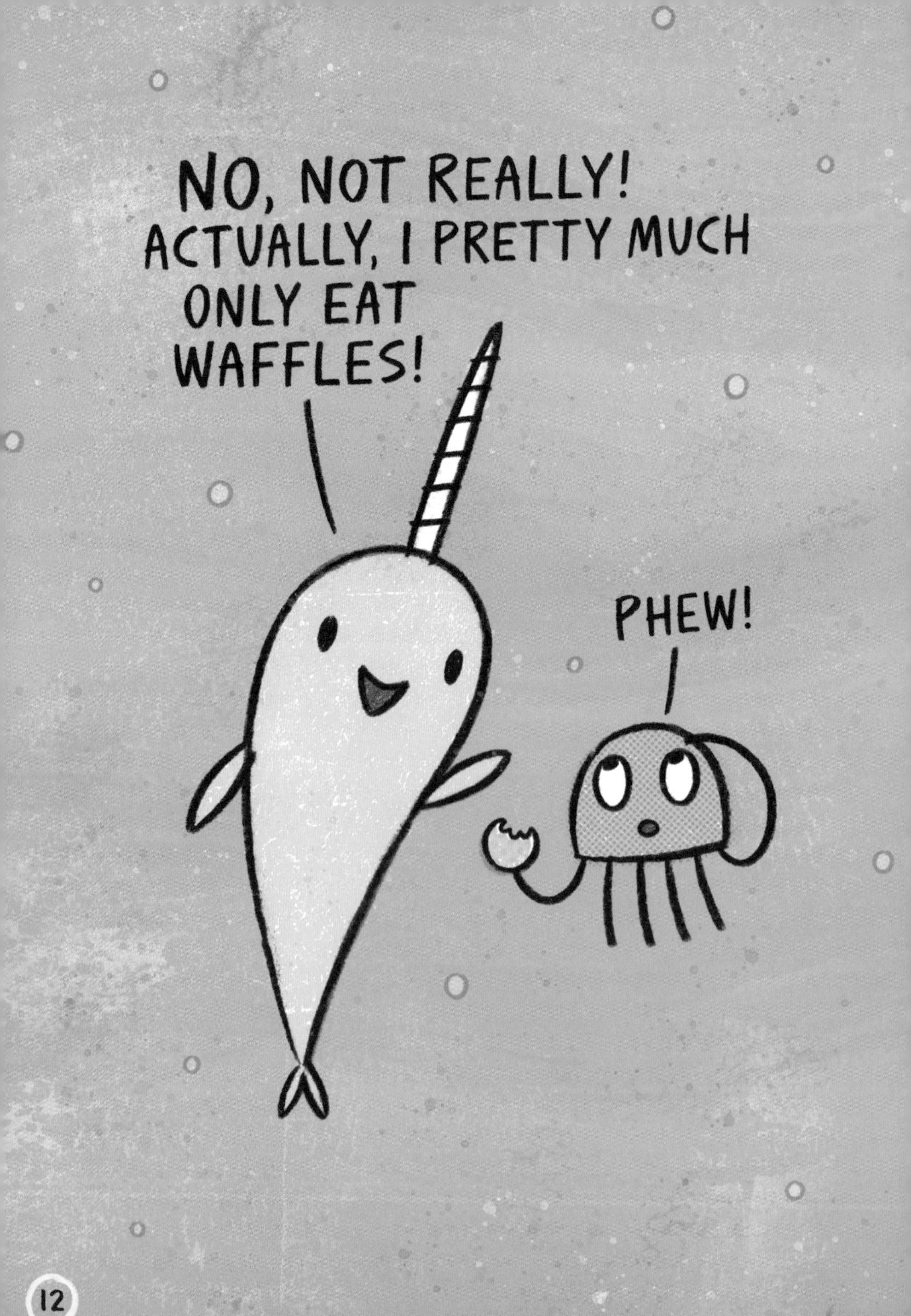
NO, NOT REALLY! ACTUALLY, I PRETTY MUCH ONLY EAT WAFFLES!
PHEW!

WAIT A MINUTE...
ONLY WAFFLES?

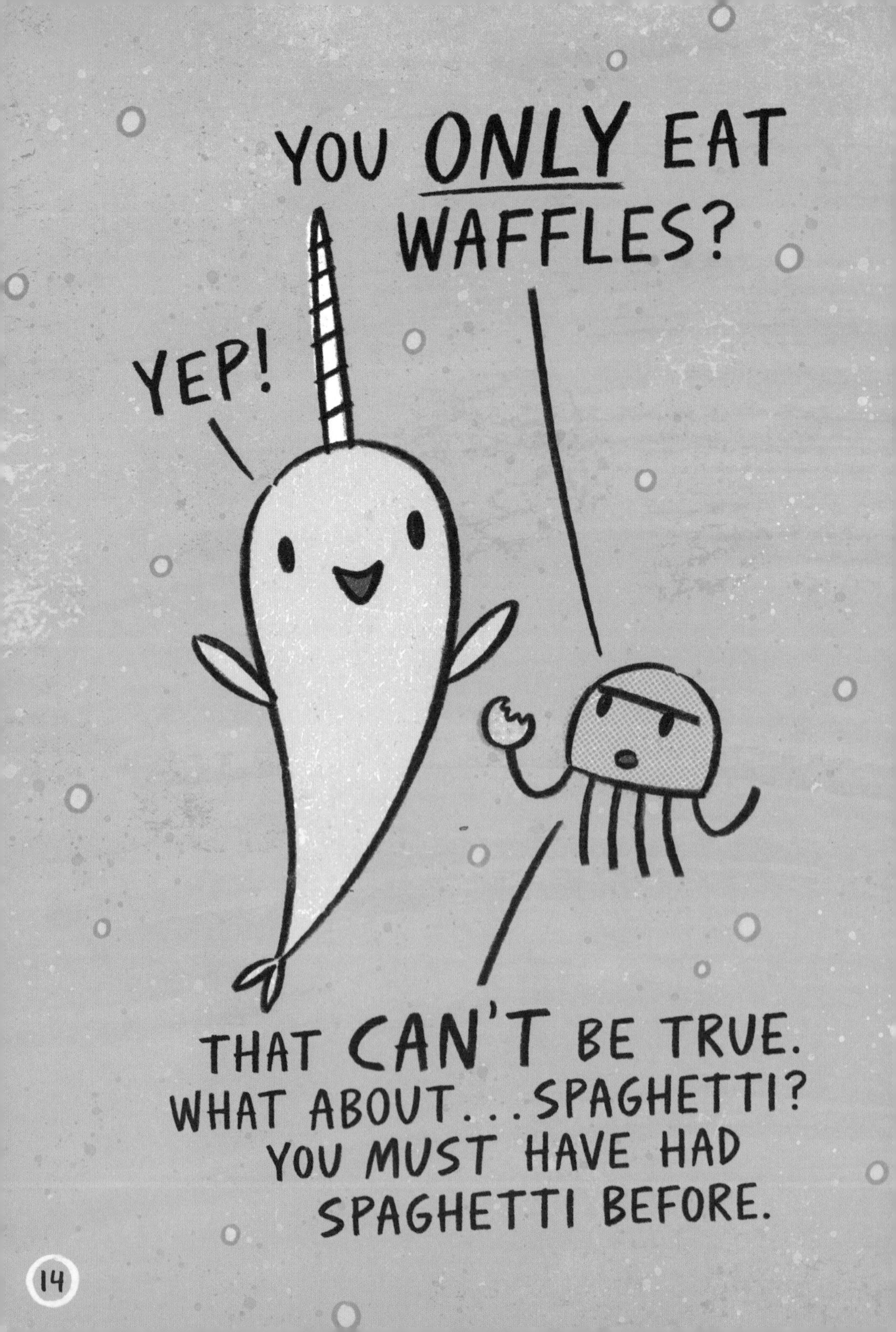
YOU ONLY EAT WAFFLES?
YEP!
THAT CAN'T BE TRUE. WHAT ABOUT...SPAGHETTI? YOU MUST HAVE HAD SPAGHETTI BEFORE.

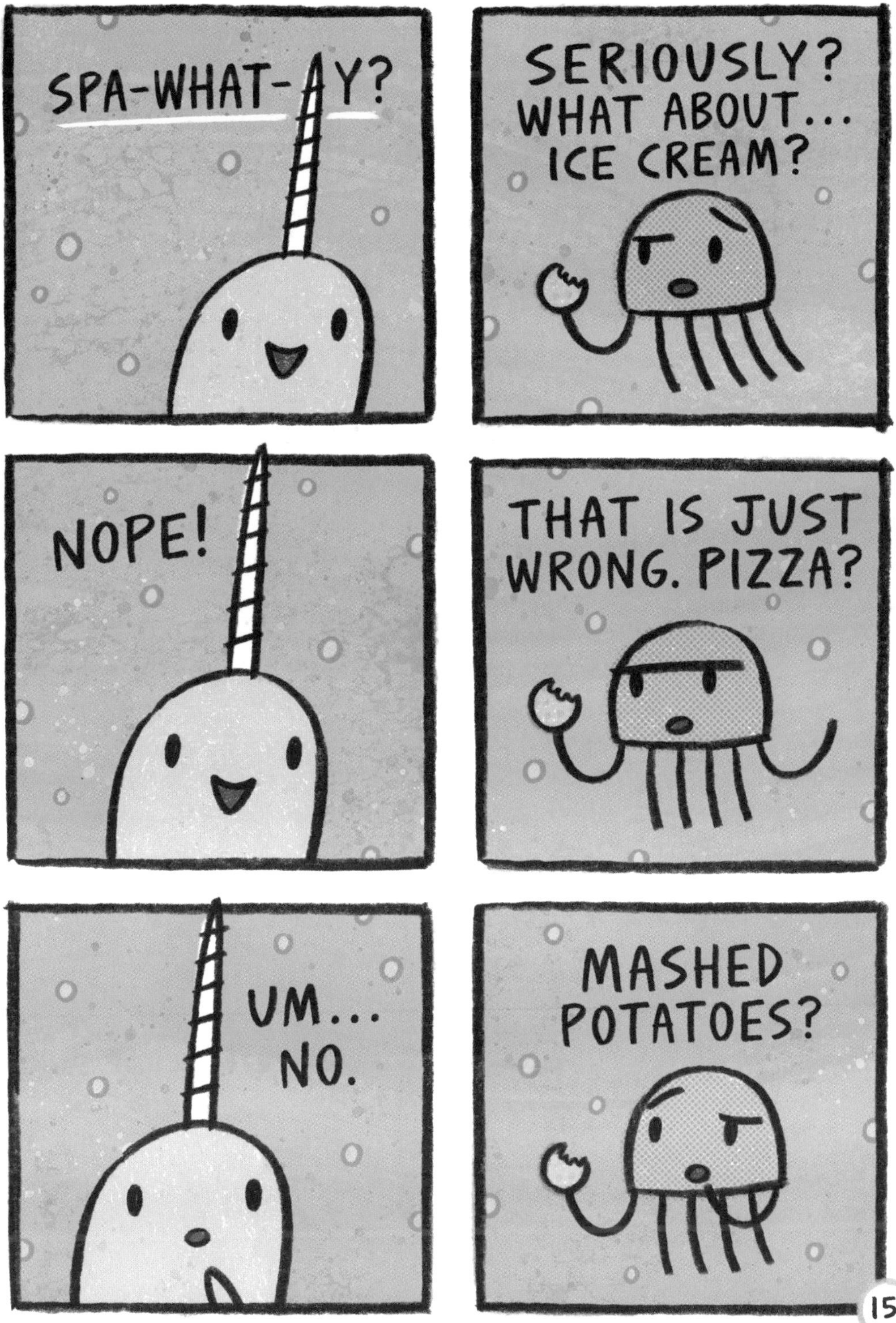
SPA-WHAT-Y?
SERIOUSLY? WHAT ABOUT... ICE CREAM?
NOPE!
THAT IS JUST WRONG. PIZZA?
UM... NO.
MASHED POTATOES?

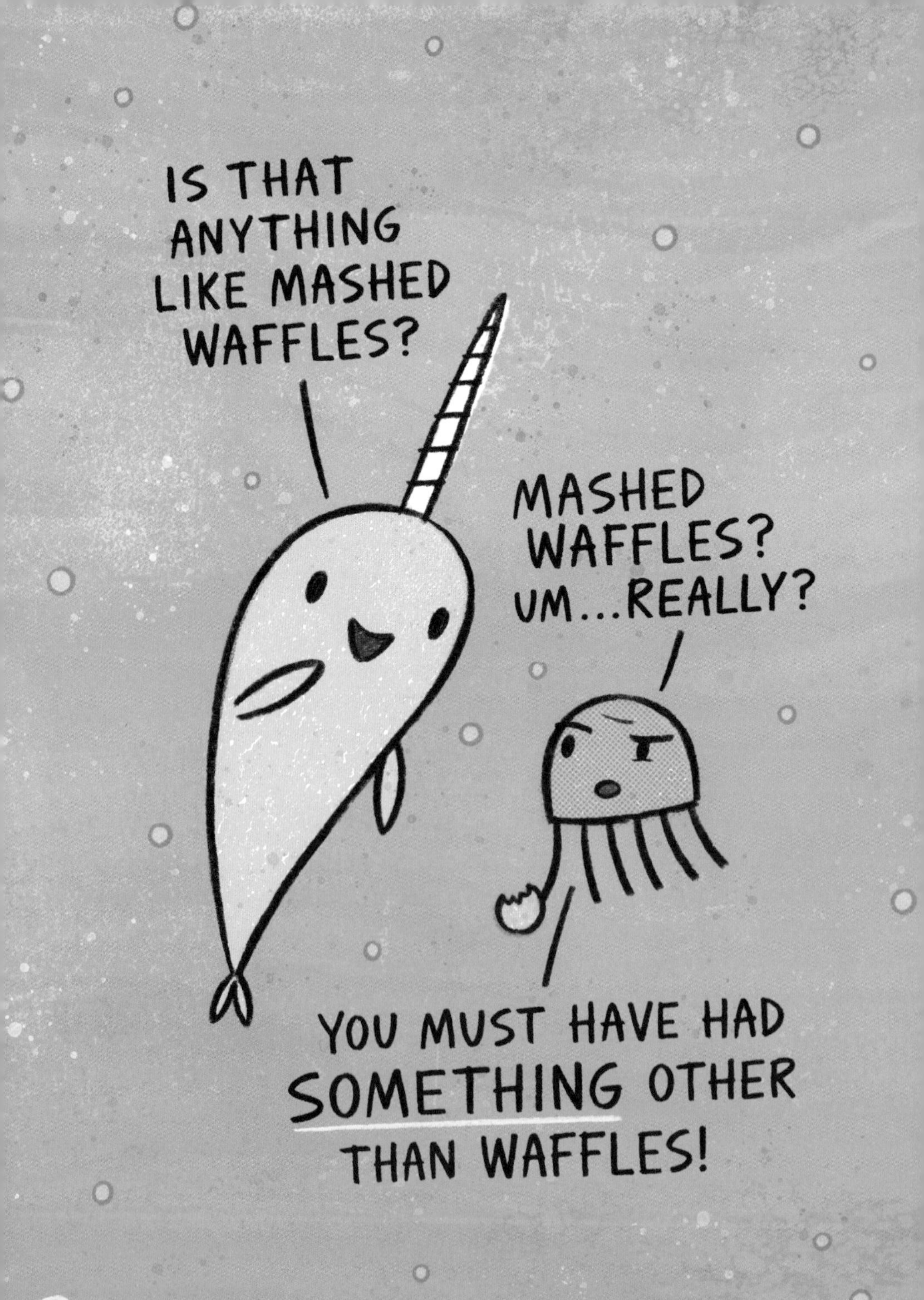
IS THAT ANYTHING LIKE MASHED WAFFLES?
MASHED WAFFLES? UM...REALLY?
YOU MUST HAVE HAD SOMETHING OTHER THAN WAFFLES!

CAKE? APPLES?
CHEESE? PIE?
ARTICHOKES?
MARSHMALLOWS?
GUACAMOLE?
UH...SUSHI?
FRENCH FRIES?

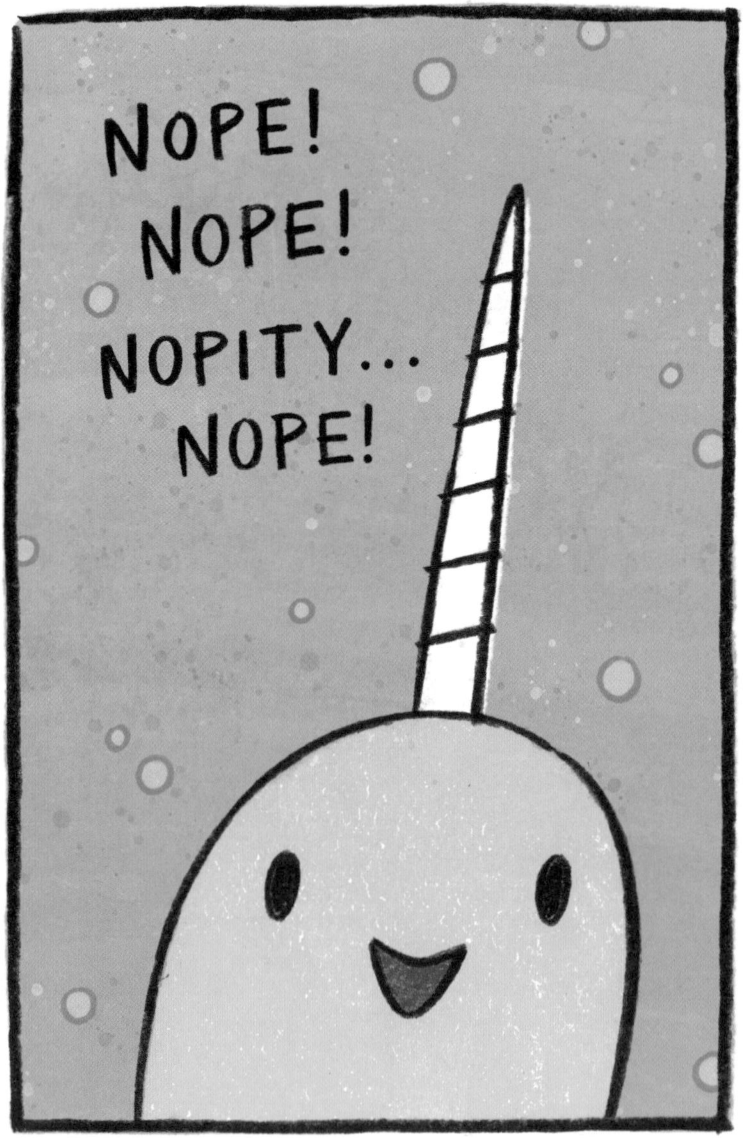
NOPE!
NOPE!
NOPITY...
NOPE!

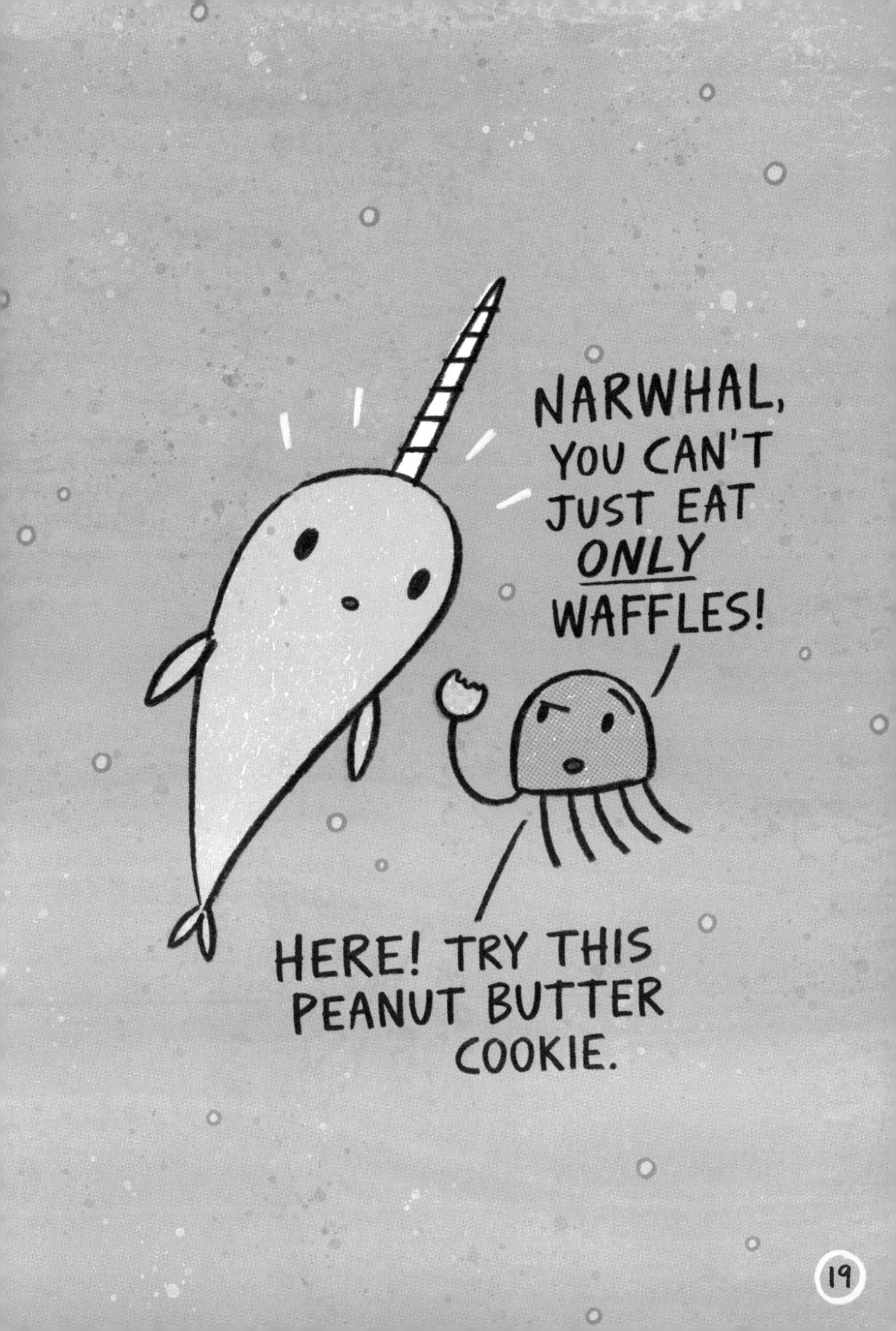
NARWHAL, YOU CAN'T JUST EAT ONLY WAFFLES!
HERE! TRY THIS PEANUT BUTTER COOKIE.

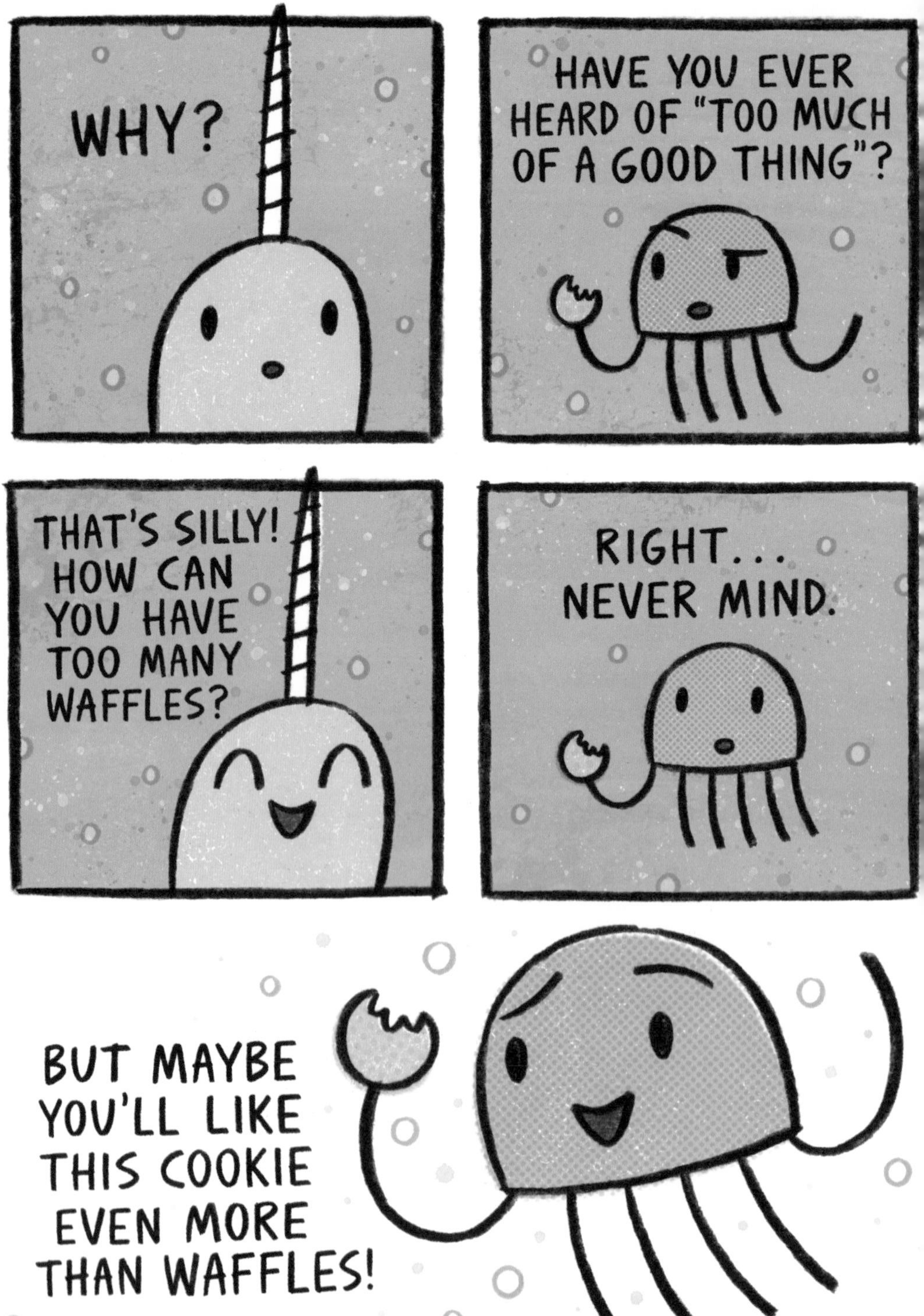
WHY?
HAVE YOU EVER HEARD OF "TOO MUCH OF A GOOD THING"?
THAT'S SILLY! HOW CAN YOU HAVE TOO MANY WAFFLES?
RIGHT.... NEVER MIND.
BUT MAYBE YOU'LL LIKE THIS COOKIE EVEN MORE THAN WAFFLES!

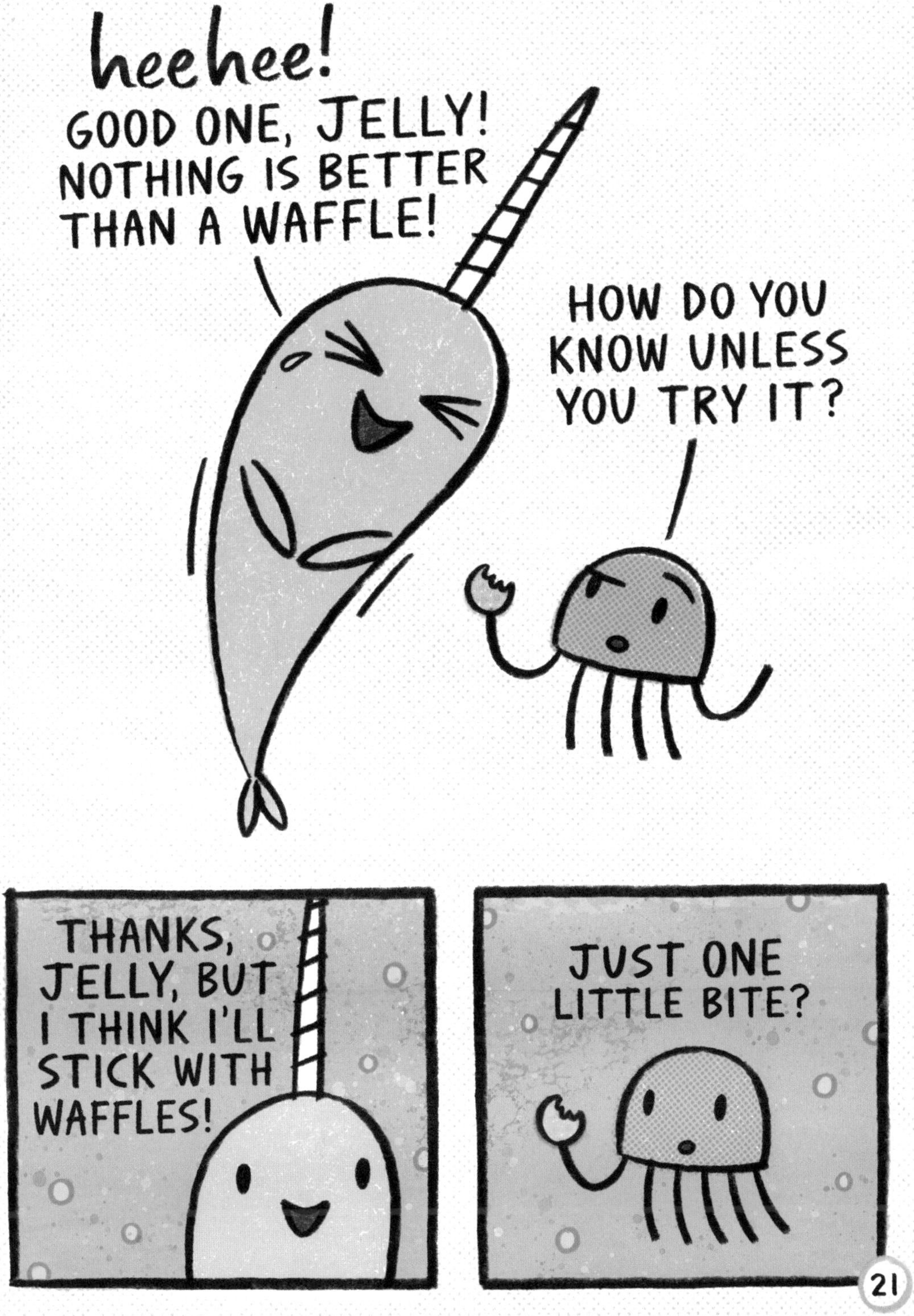
heehee!
GOOD ONE, JELLY! NOTHING IS BETTER THAN A WAFFLE!
HOW DO YOU KNOW UNLESS YOU TRY IT?
THANKS, JELLY, BUT I THINK I'LL STICK WITH WAFFLES!
JUST ONE LITTLE BITE?

I TELL YOU WHAT,
I'LL MAKE YOU AN
EXTRA LARGE
WAFFLE IF YOU JUST
TRY THIS PEANUT
BUTTER COOKIE.

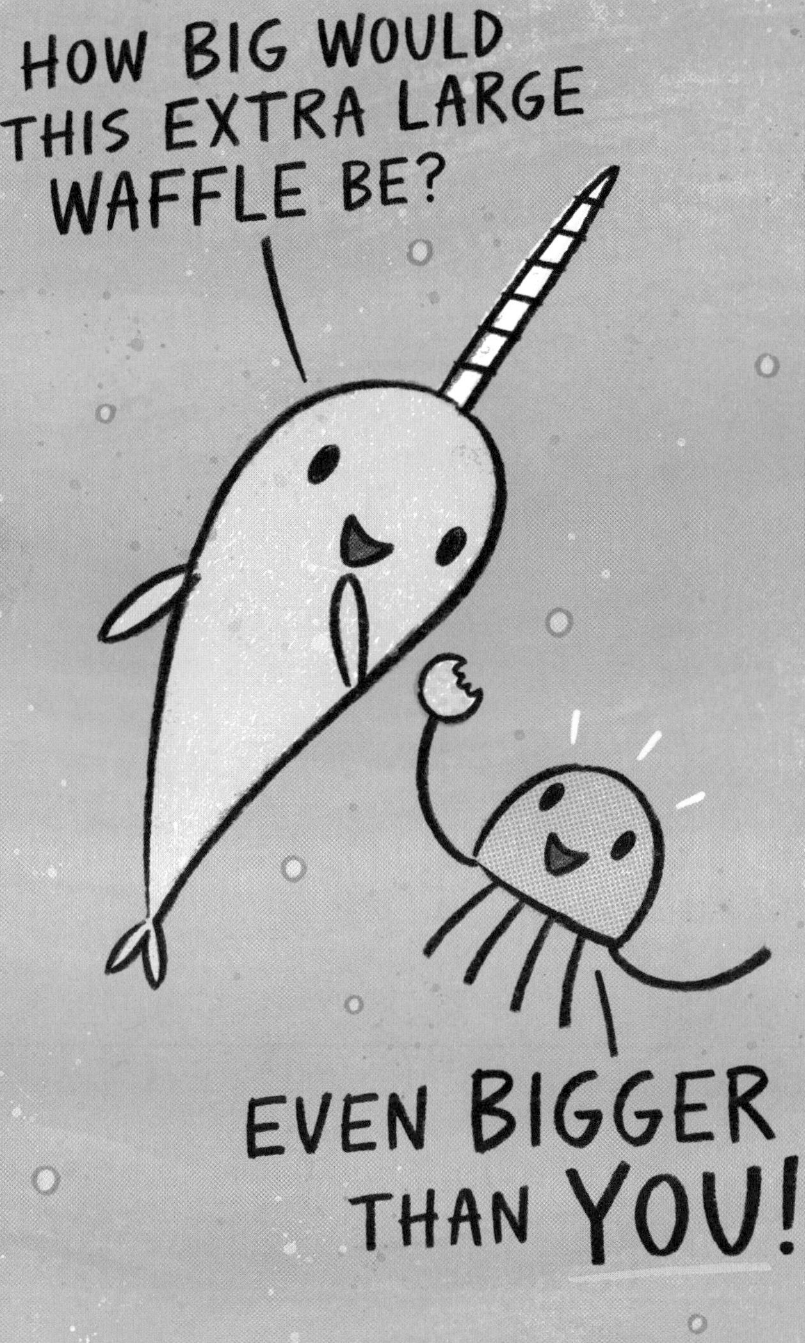
HOW BIG WOULD THIS EXTRA LARGE WAFFLE BE?
EVEN BIGGER THAN YOU!

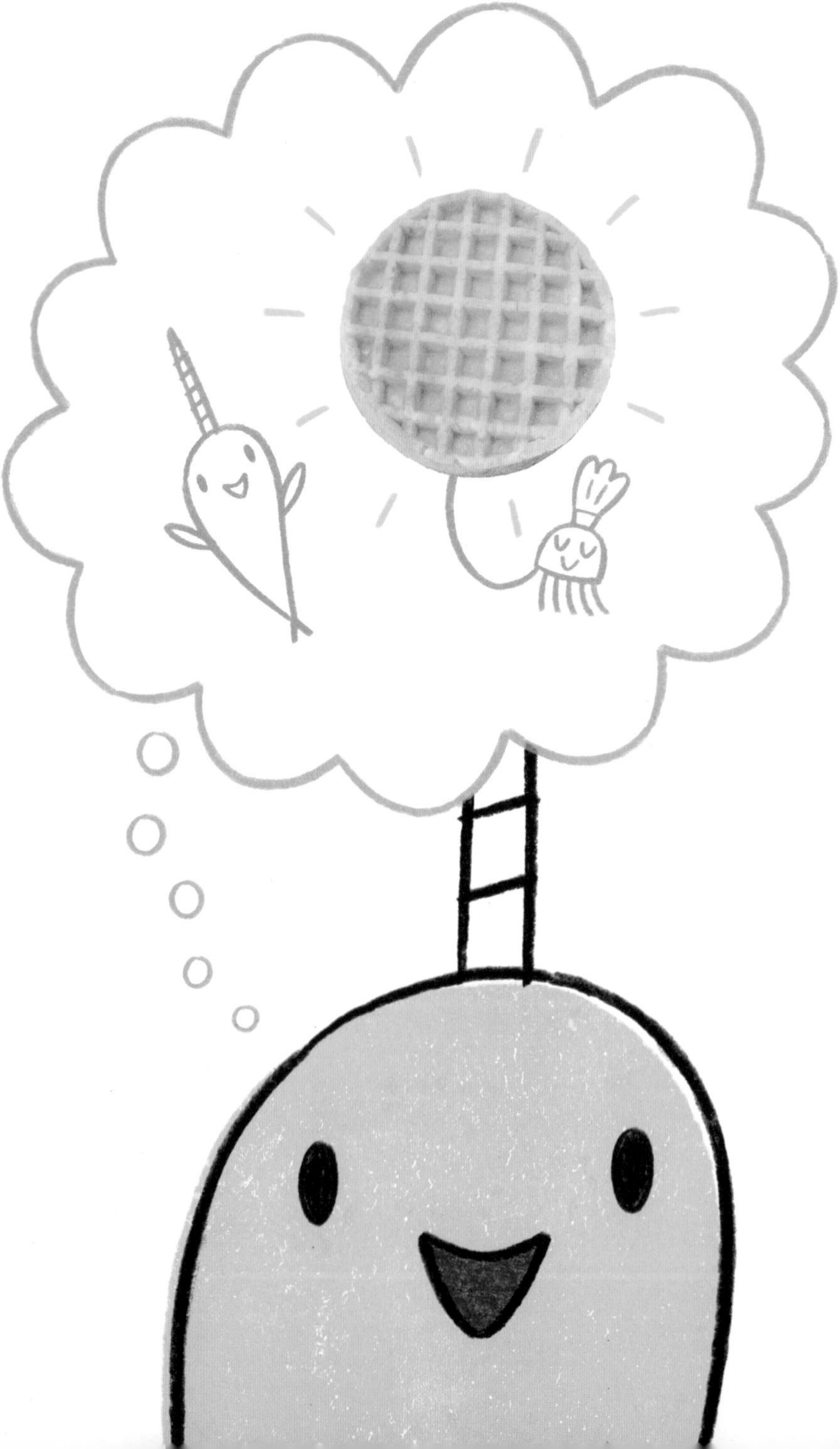

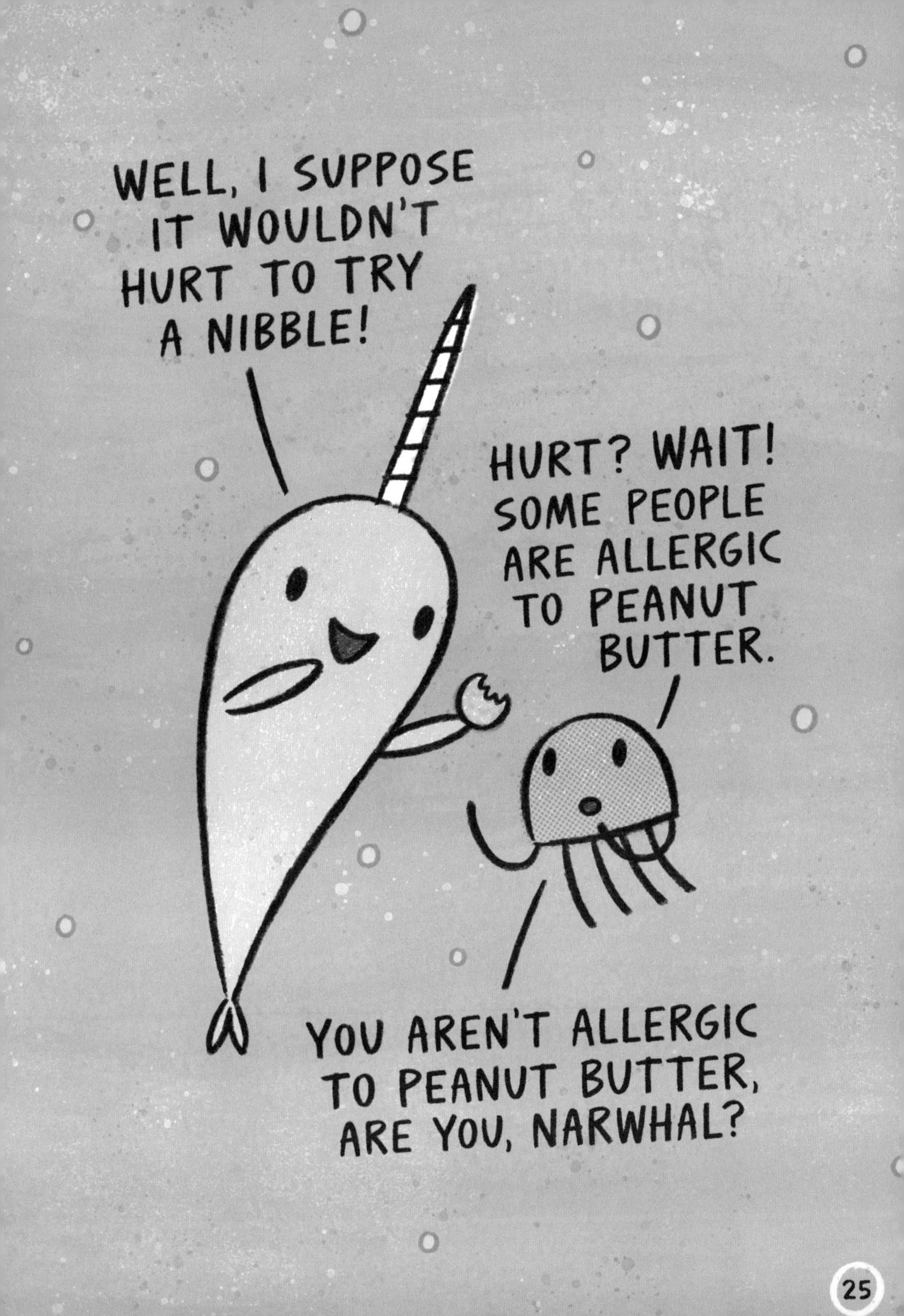
WELL, I SUPPOSE IT WOULDN'T HURT TO TRY A NIBBLE!
HURT? WAIT! SOME PEOPLE ARE ALLERGIC TO PEANUT BUTTER.
YOU AREN'T ALLERGIC TO PEANUT BUTTER, ARE YOU, NARWHAL?

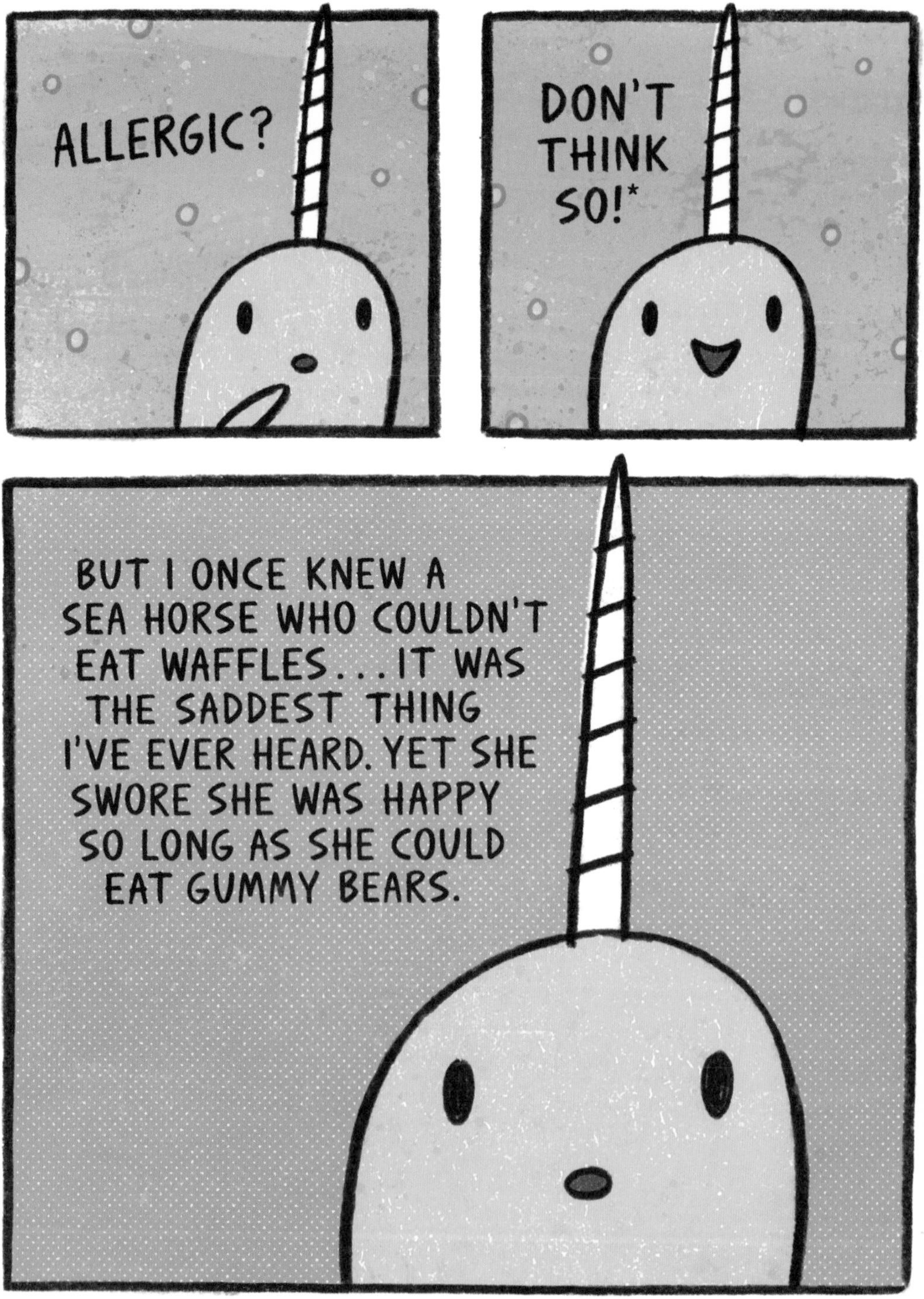
ALLERGIC?
DON'T THINK SO!*
BUT I ONCE KNEW A SEA HORSE WHO COULDN'T EAT WAFFLES...IT WAS THE SADDEST THING I'VE EVER HEARD. YET SHE SWORE SHE WAS HAPPY SO LONG AS SHE COULD EAT GUMMY BEARS.

*THE ALLERGIC AQUATIC ANIMALS AWARENESS ASSOCIATION ADVISES CAUTION WHEN TRYING A COMMON ALLERGEN.

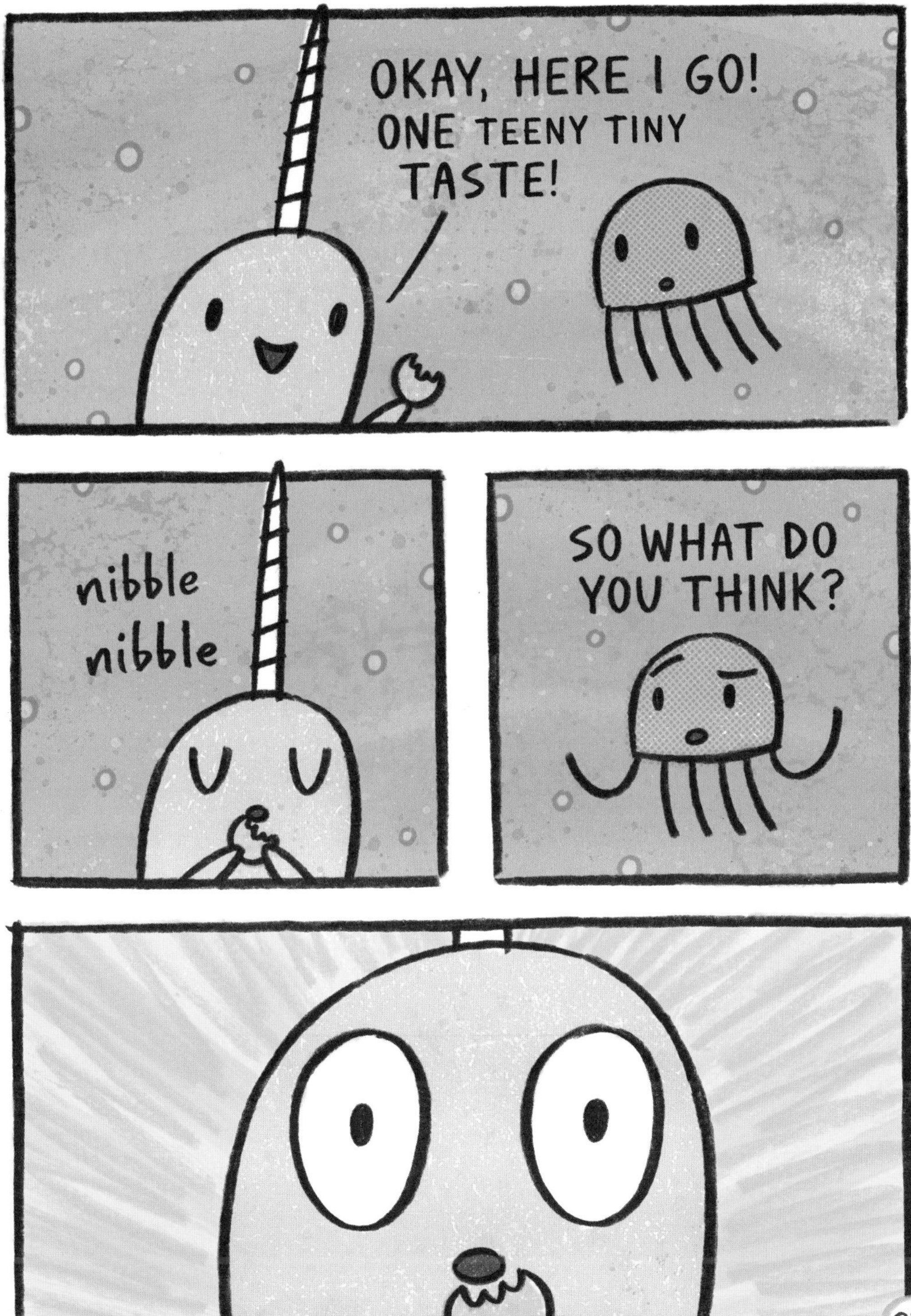
OKAY, HERE I GO! ONE TEENY TINY TASTE!
nibble nibble
SO WHAT DO YOU THINK?

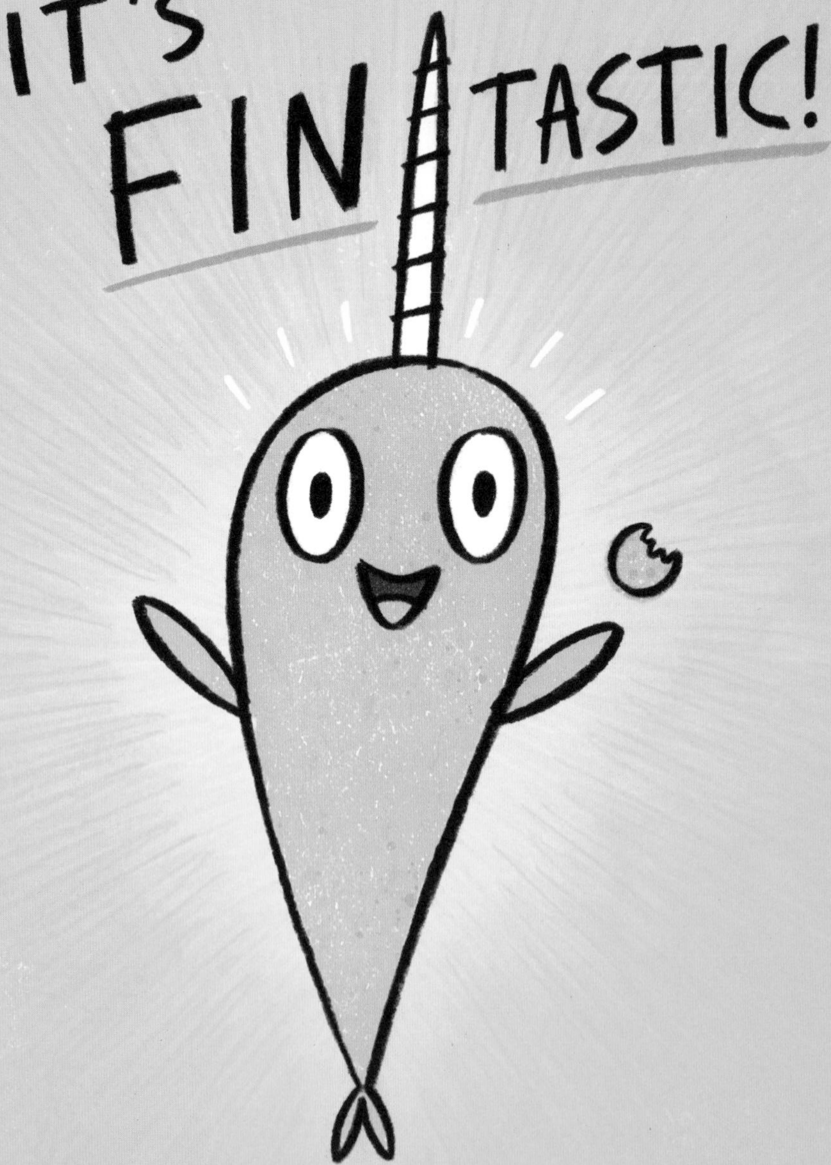
IT'S
FIN TASTIC!

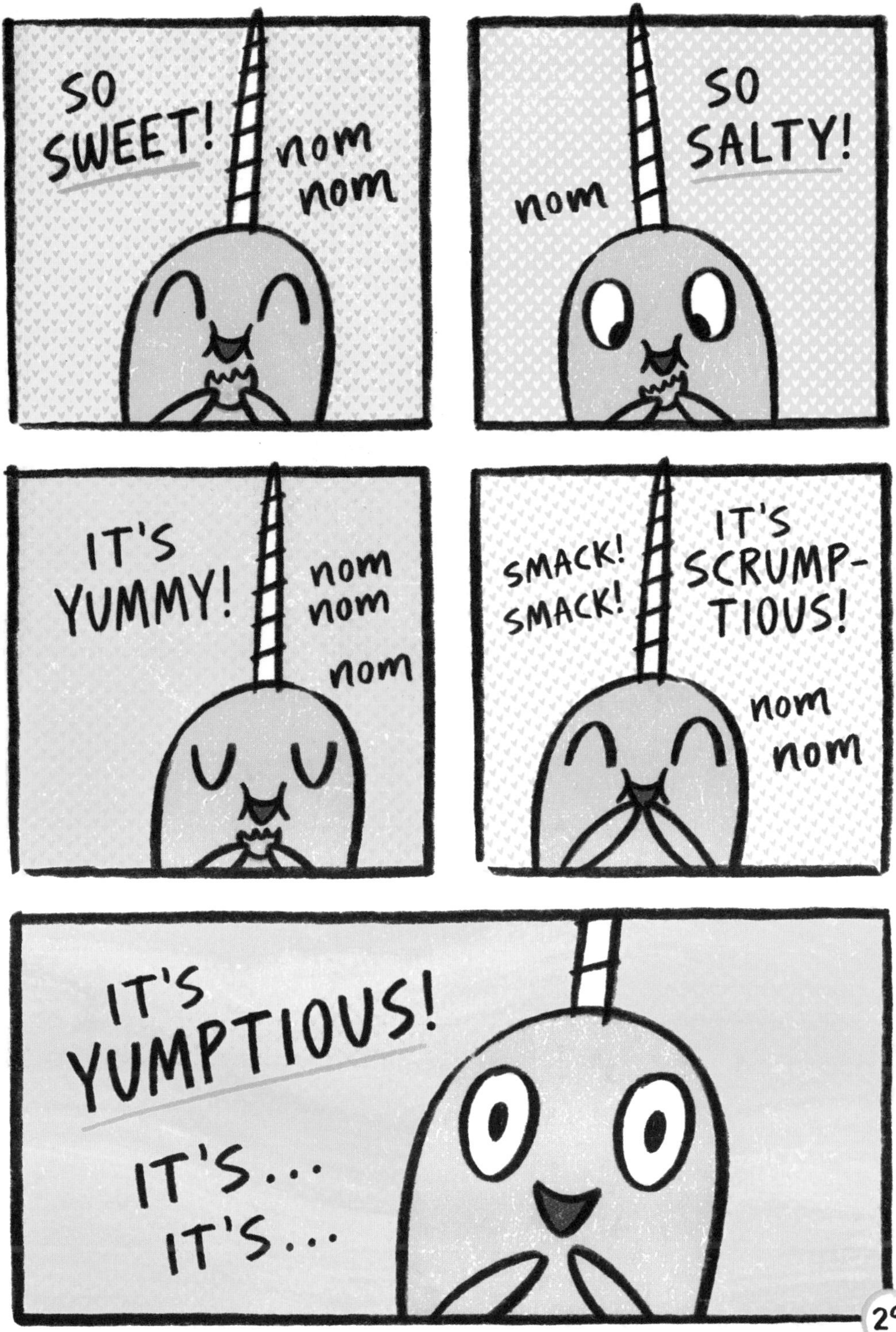
SO SWEET!
nom nom
SO SALTY!
nom
IT'S YUMMY!
nom nom
nom
SMACK! SMACK!
IT'S SCRUMP-TIOUS!
nom nom
IT'S YUMPTIOUS!
IT'S...
IT'S...

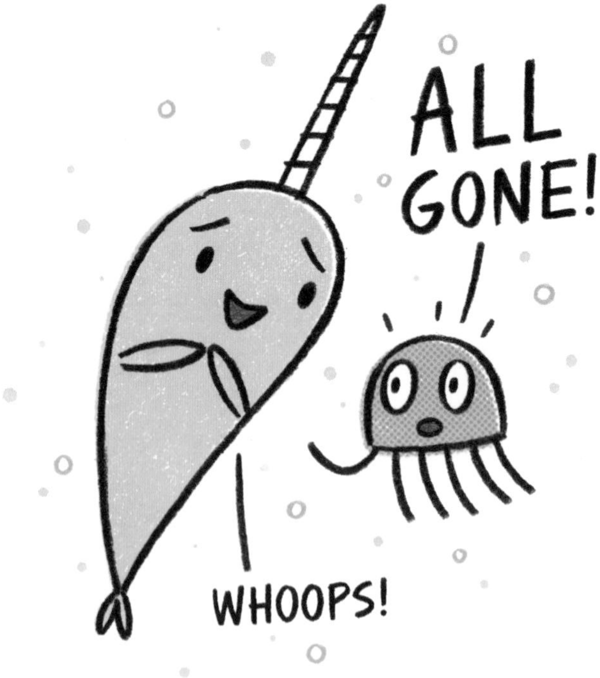
ALL GONE!
WHOOPS!

DELICIOUS FACTS

SCIENTISTS BELIEVE NARWHALS SUCK UP THEIR FOOD WHOLE AND EAT MAINLY FISH.

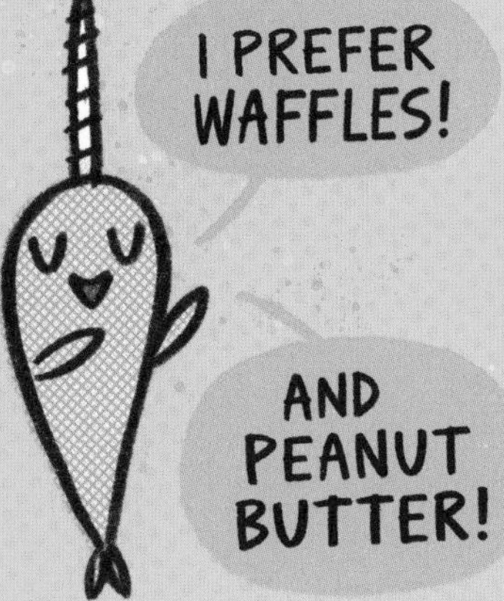
I PREFER WAFFLES!
AND PEANUT BUTTER!

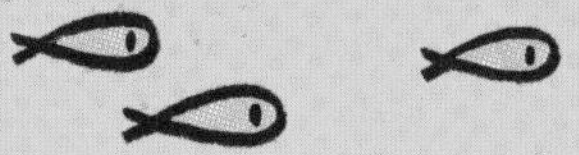

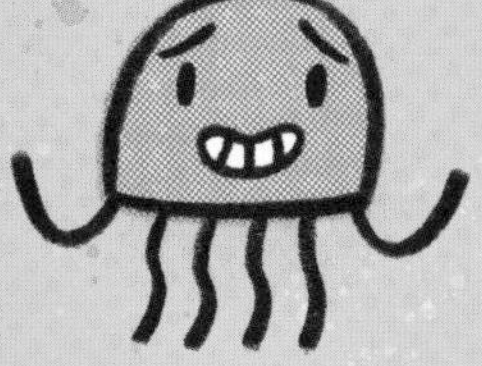

MOST JELLYFISH STING THEIR PREY WITH THEIR TENTACLES BEFORE EATING IT.

BLUE WHALES (THE LARGEST ANIMAL EVER) EAT MAINLY TINY LITTLE KRILL. THEY EAT OODLES OF THEM. AS MANY AS 40 MILLION KRILL PER DAY!

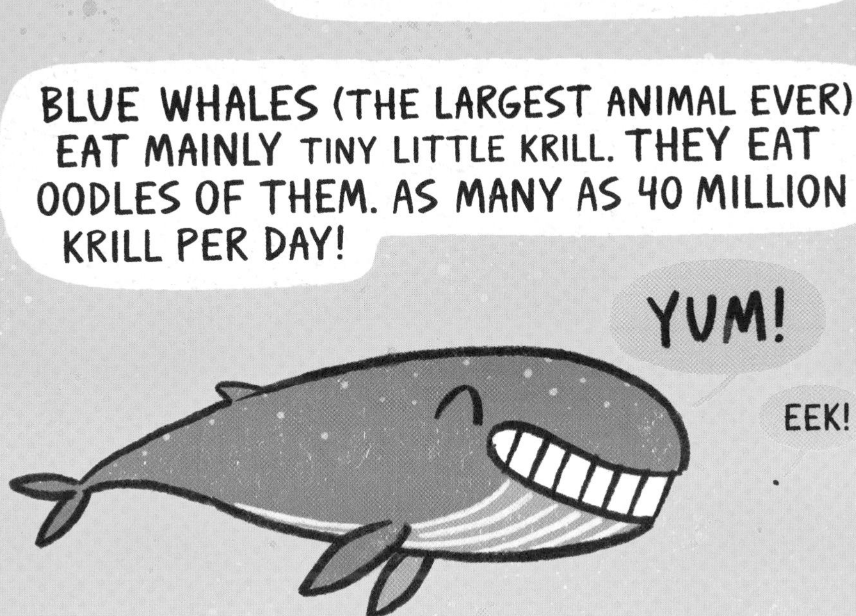
YUM!
EEK!

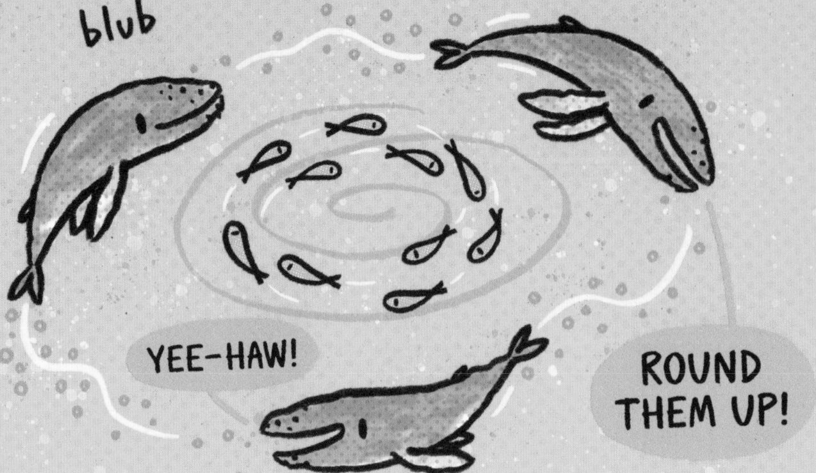
blub
YEE-HAW!
ROUND THEM UP!

HUMPBACK WHALES WORK TOGETHER TO CREATE COMPLEX BUBBLE NETS TO CORRAL FISH TO EAT.

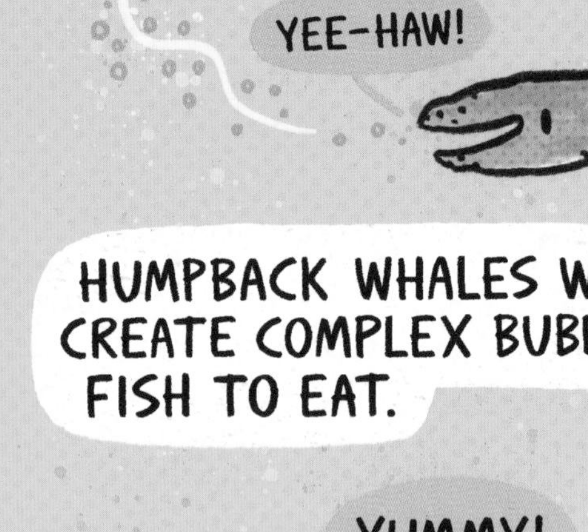
YUMMY!

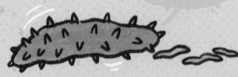

SEA CUCUMBERS EAT ALL SORTS OF THINGS, INCLUDING POOP.

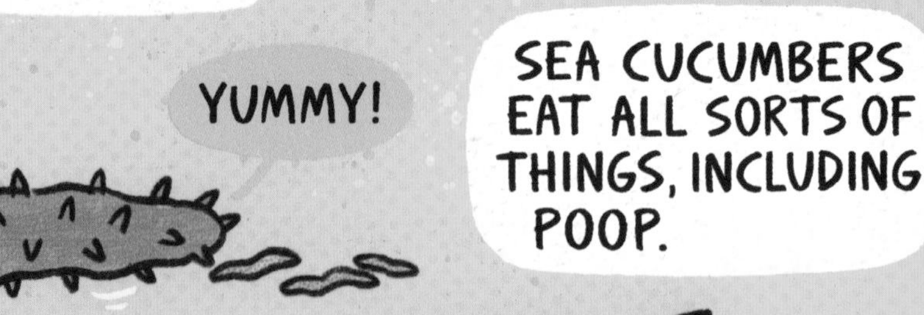
I'VE GOT A TUMMY ACHE!

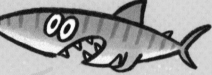

TIGER SHARKS ARE OFTEN REFERRED TO AS "THE TRASH CANS OF THE SEA" BECAUSE THEY WILL EAT JUST ABOUT ANYTHING, FROM PIGS TO TIRES TO EXPLOSIVES.

AHOY, PEANUT BUTTER?

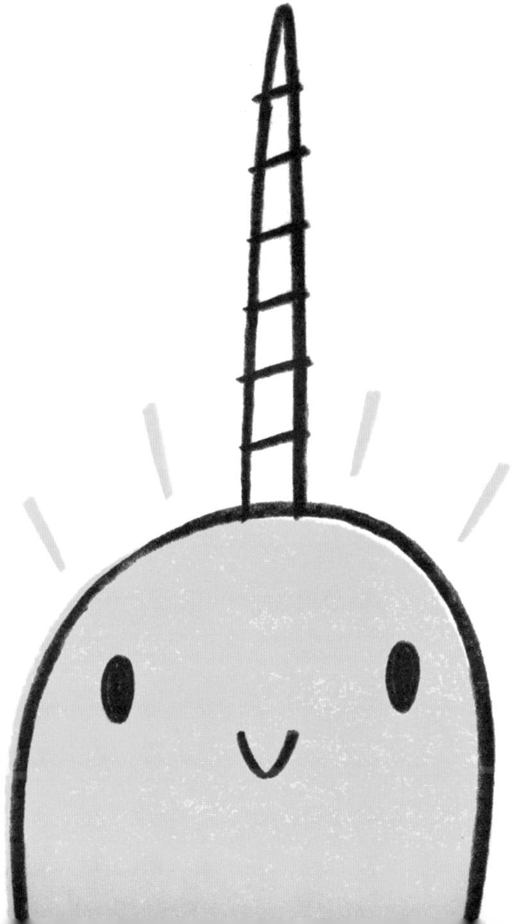

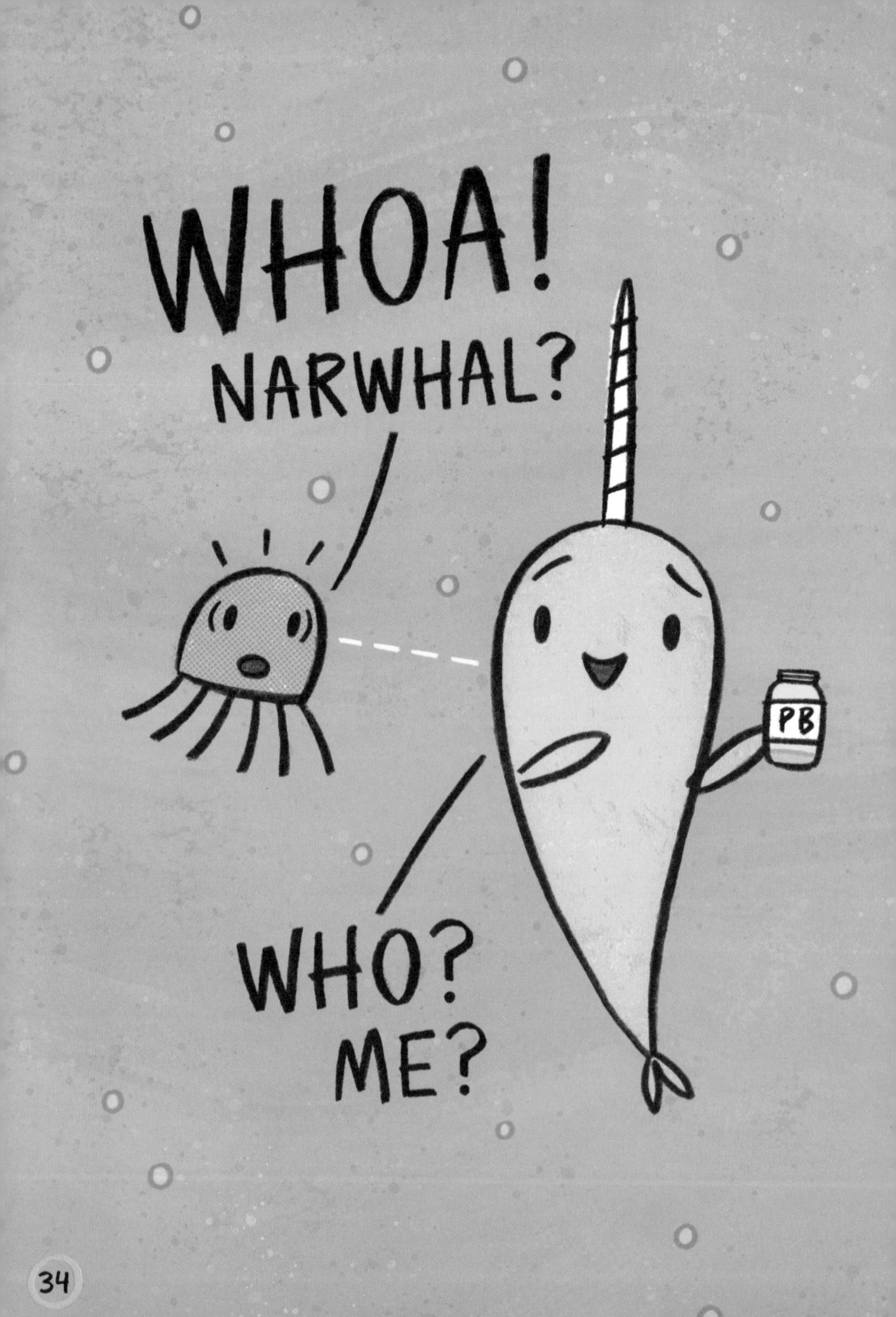
WHOA!
NARWHAL?
WHO?
ME?
PB

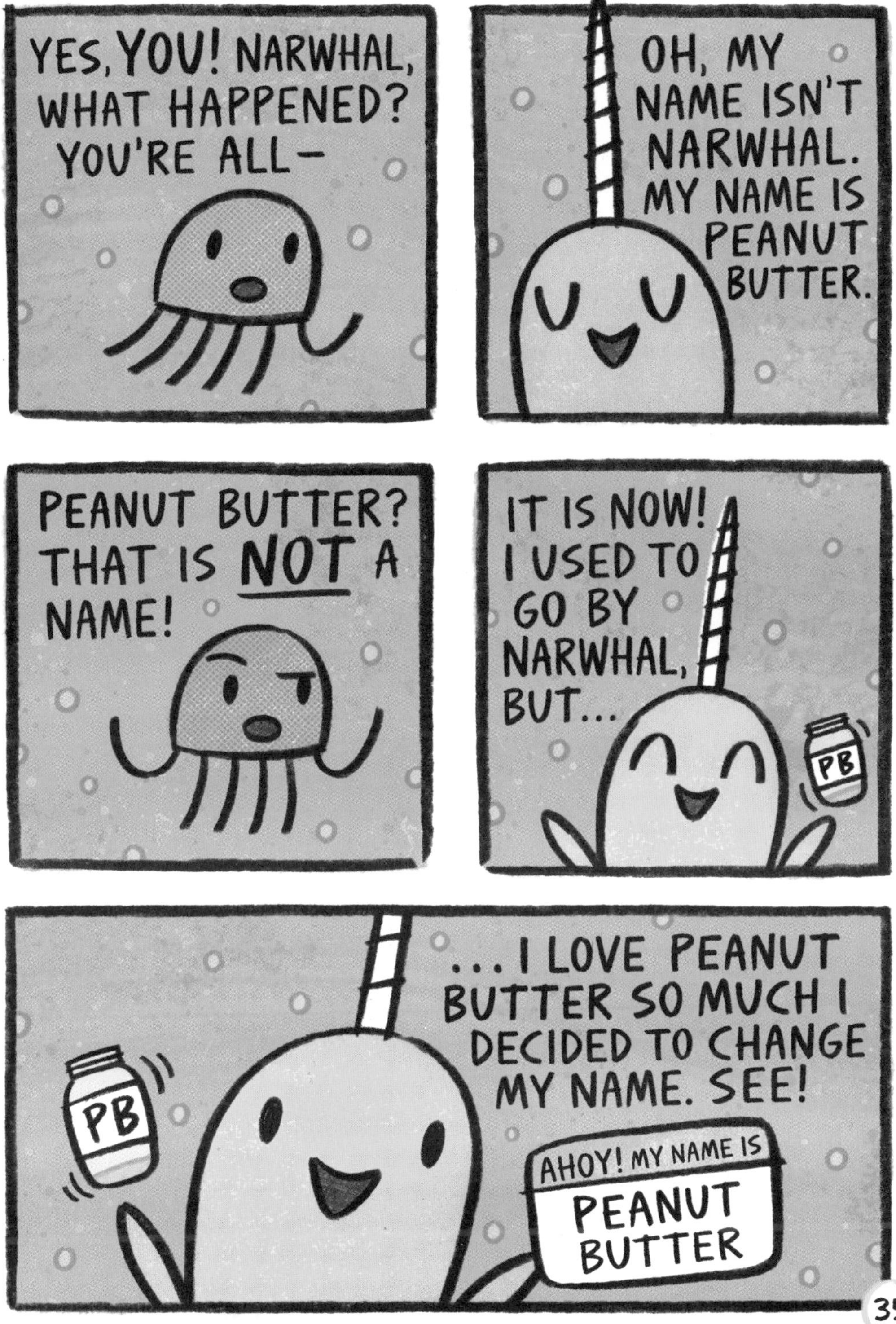
YES, YOU! NARWHAL, WHAT HAPPENED? YOU'RE ALL–
OH, MY NAME ISN'T NARWHAL. MY NAME IS PEANUT BUTTER.
PEANUT BUTTER? THAT IS NOT A NAME!
IT IS NOW! I USED TO GO BY NARWHAL, BUT...
PB
...I LOVE PEANUT BUTTER SO MUCH I DECIDED TO CHANGE MY NAME. SEE!
PB
AHOY! MY NAME IS
PEANUT BUTTER

WHAT? YOU CAN'T JUST CHANGE YOUR NAME!

WHY NOT?

BECAUSE! IT ISN'T NORMAL!

OH.

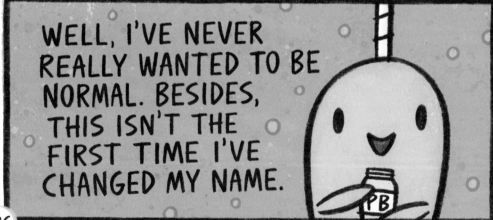

WELL, I'VE NEVER REALLY WANTED TO BE NORMAL. BESIDES, THIS ISN'T THE FIRST TIME I'VE CHANGED MY NAME.

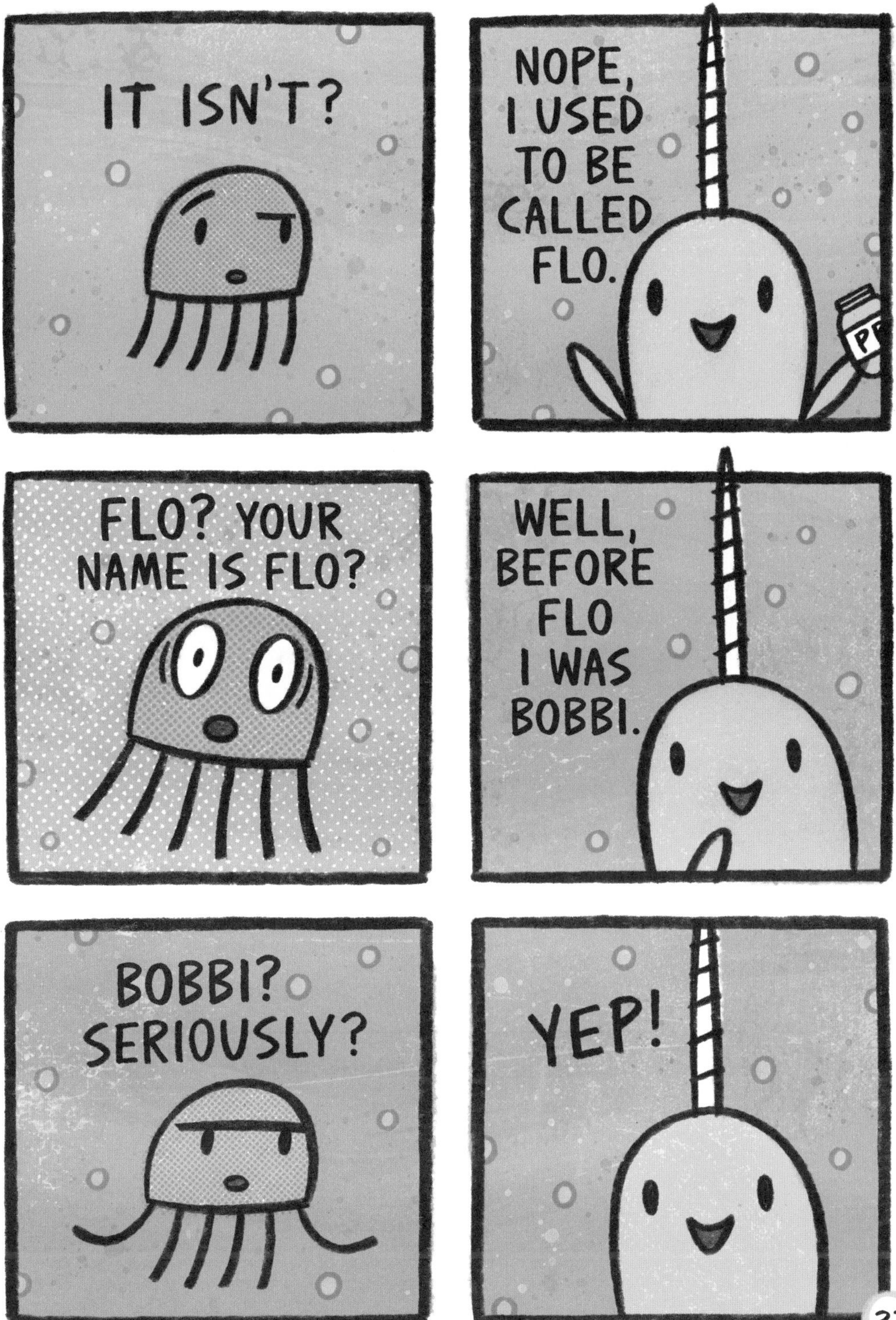
IT ISN'T?
NOPE, I USED TO BE CALLED FLO.
FLO? YOUR NAME IS FLO?
WELL, BEFORE FLO I WAS BOBBI.
BOBBI? SERIOUSLY?
YEP!

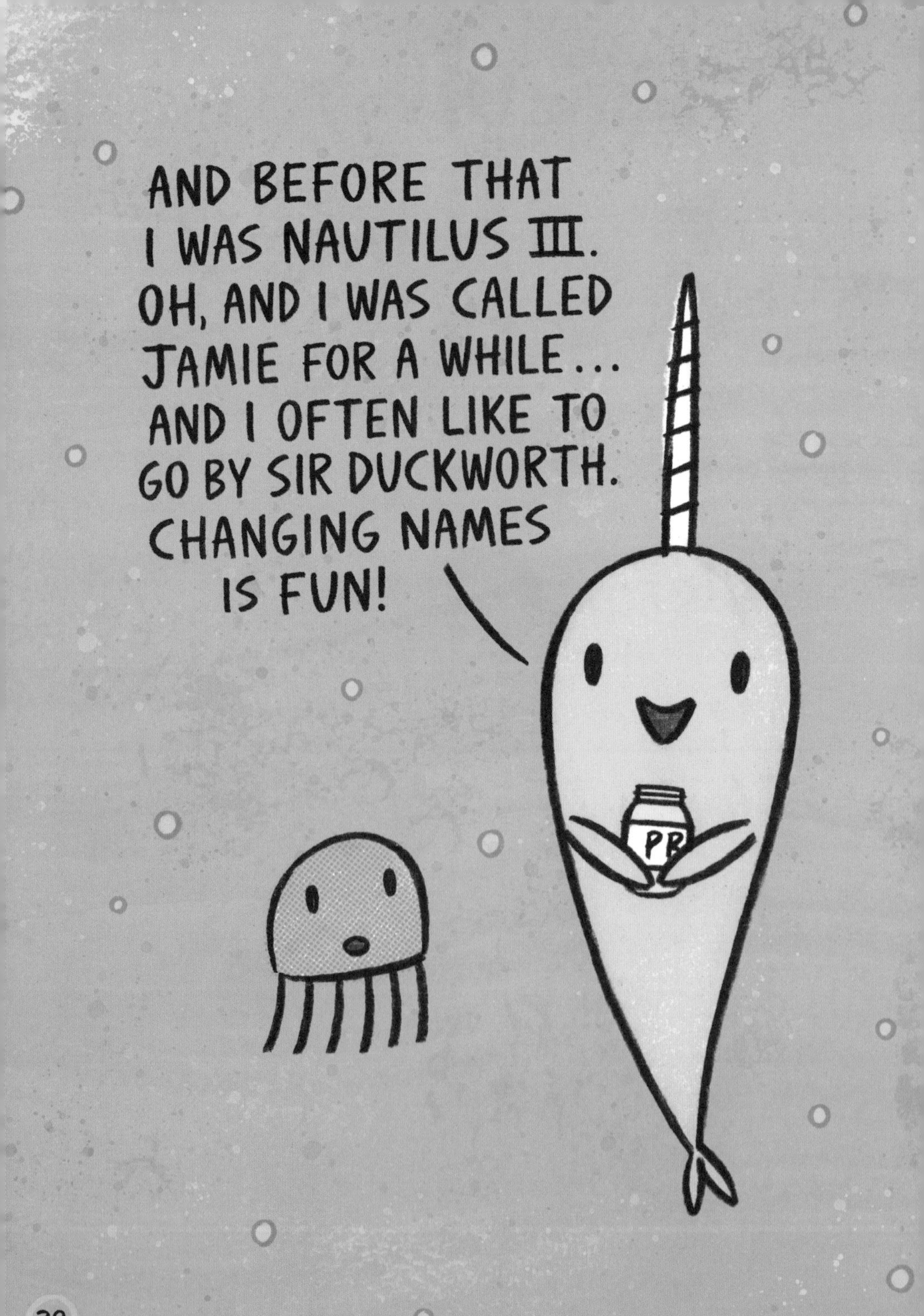
AND BEFORE THAT I WAS NAUTILUS III. OH, AND I WAS CALLED JAMIE FOR A WHILE... AND I OFTEN LIKE TO GO BY SIR DUCKWORTH. CHANGING NAMES IS FUN!
PB

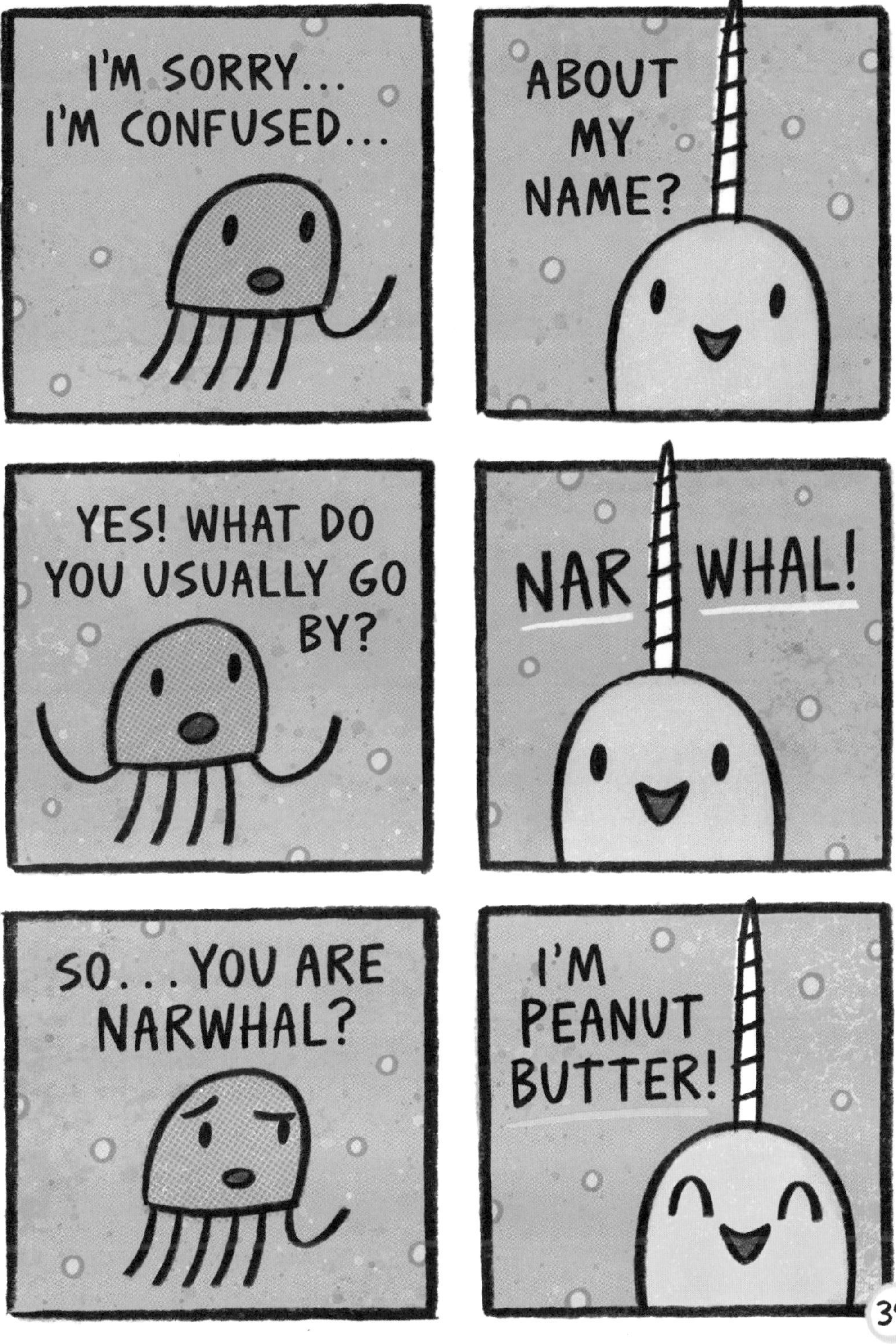
I'M SORRY...
I'M CONFUSED...
ABOUT MY NAME?
YES! WHAT DO YOU USUALLY GO BY?
NAR WHAL!
SO... YOU ARE NARWHAL?
I'M PEANUT BUTTER!

WOW,
YOU MUST
REALLY LIKE
PEANUT BUTTER
THEN!

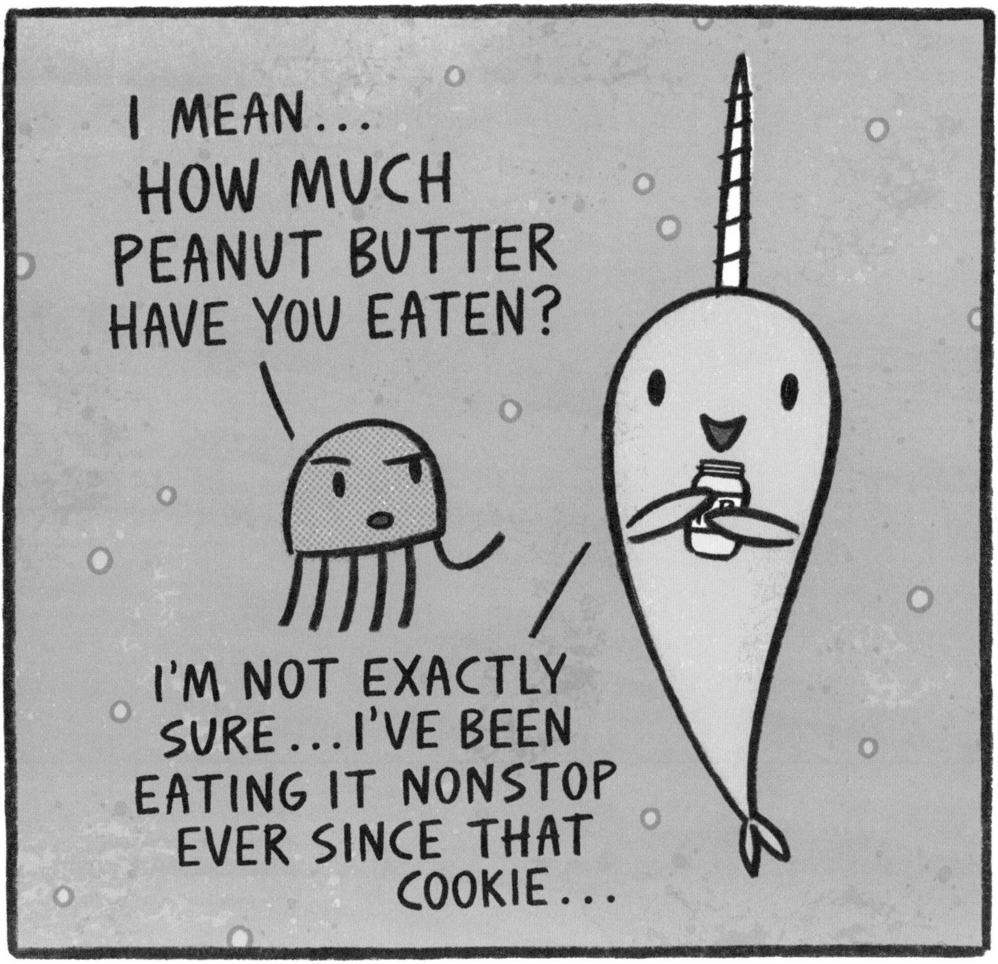
I MEAN... HOW MUCH PEANUT BUTTER HAVE YOU EATEN?
I'M NOT EXACTLY SURE...I'VE BEEN EATING IT NONSTOP EVER SINCE THAT COOKIE...

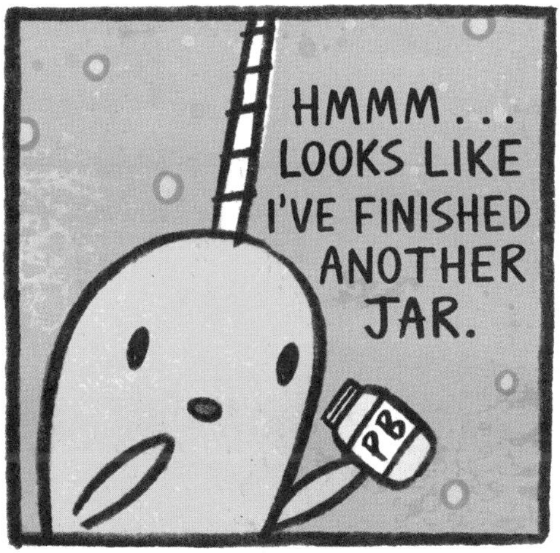
HMMM... LOOKS LIKE I'VE FINISHED ANOTHER JAR.
PB

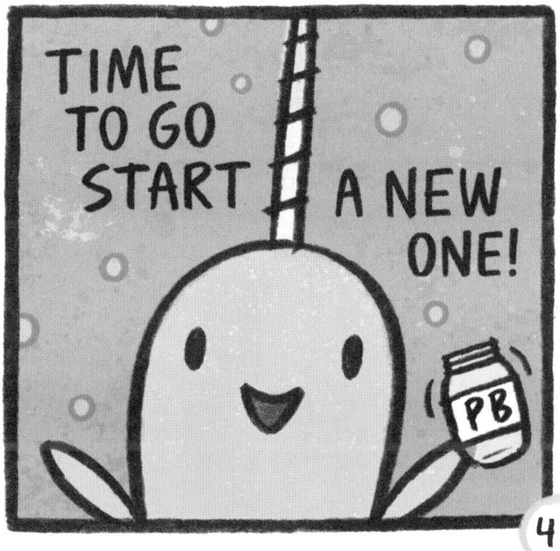
TIME TO GO START
A NEW ONE!
PB

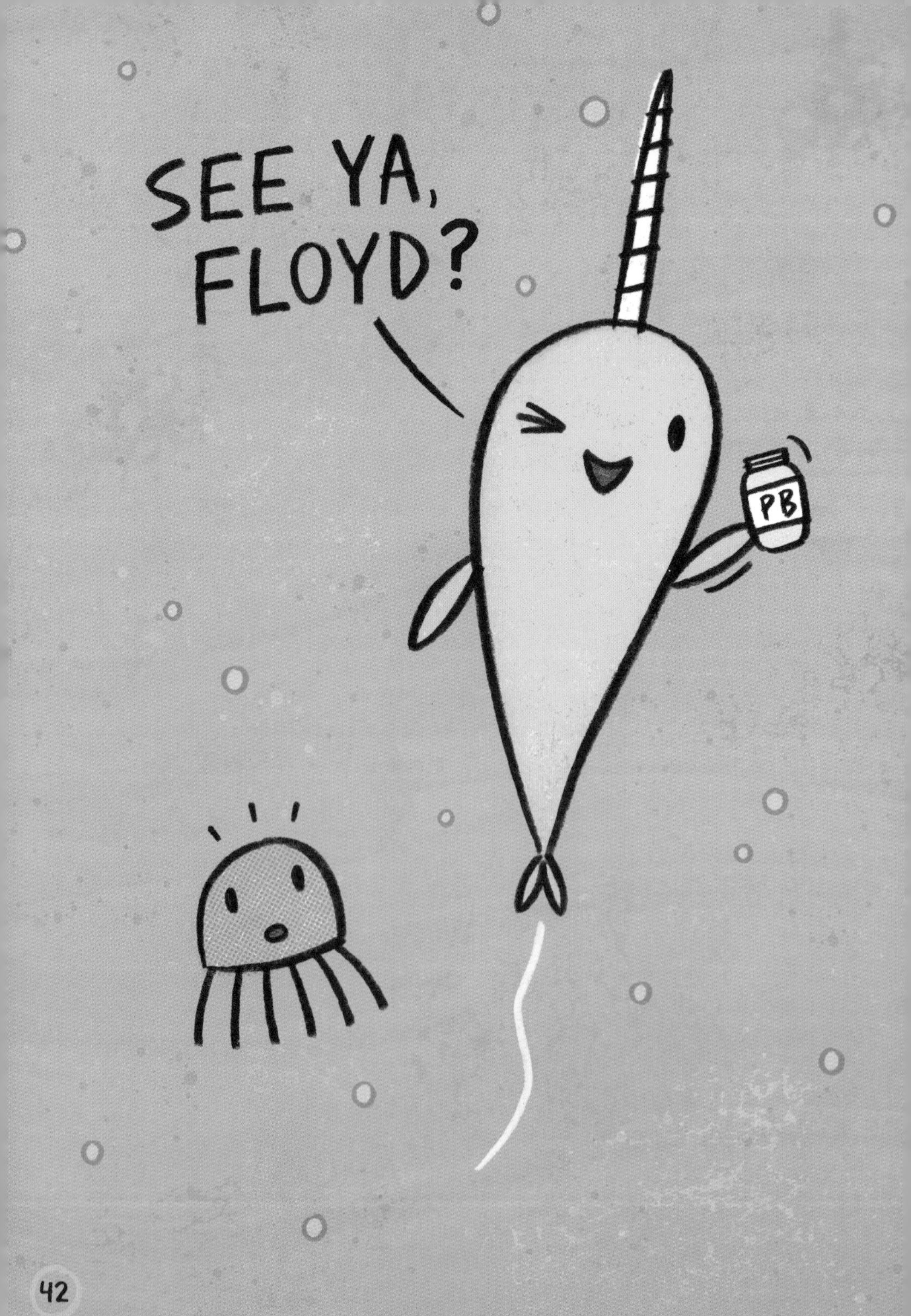
SEE YA, FLOYD?
PB

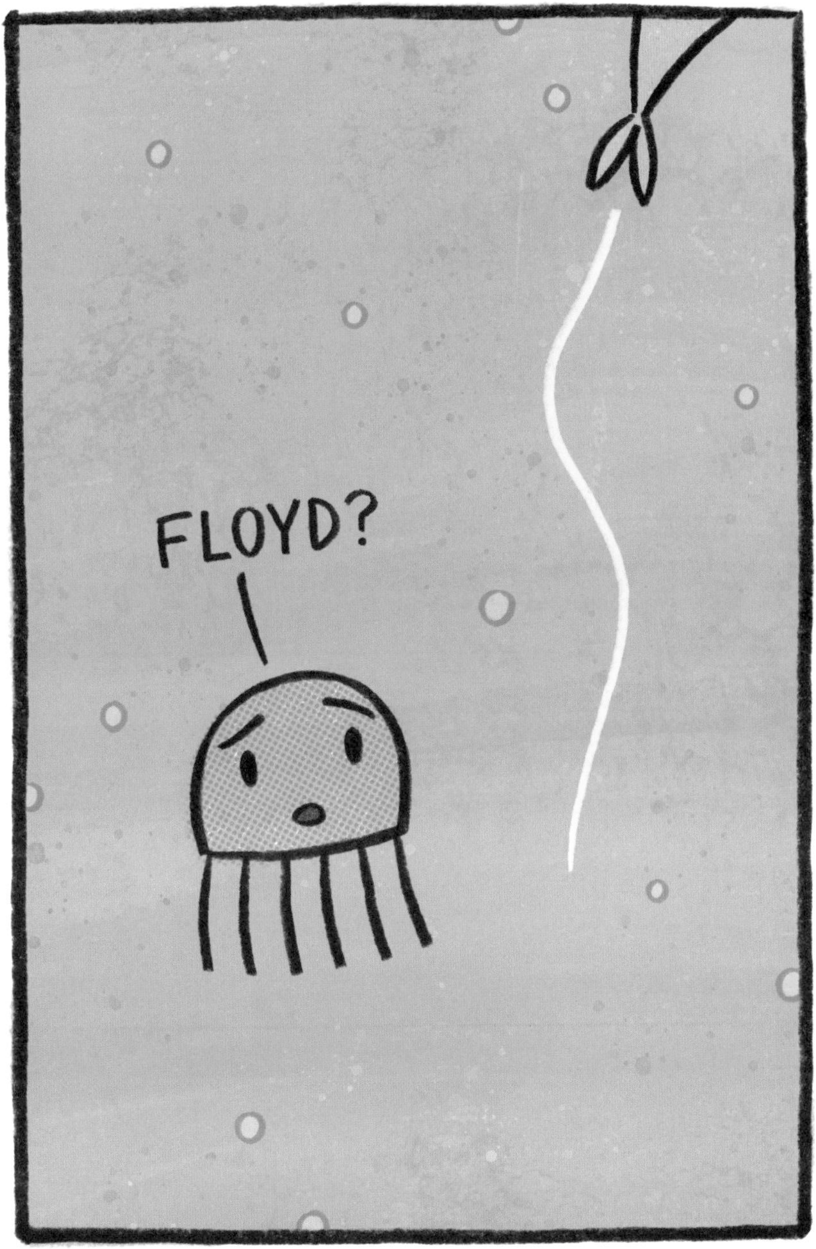
FLOYD?

FLOYD...

SUPER WAFFLE
AND STRAWBERRY SIDEKICK
VS. PB&J

Peanut Butter   Floyd
by ~~Narwhal~~ and ~~Jelly~~

SUPER WAFFLE AND
STRAWBERRY SIDEKICK
HAVE BEATEN ANGRY
ROBOTS AND VILLAINOUS
BLOBS, SO THIS PICKLE
WILL BE A PIECE OF CAKE
...PIECE OF PICKLE?

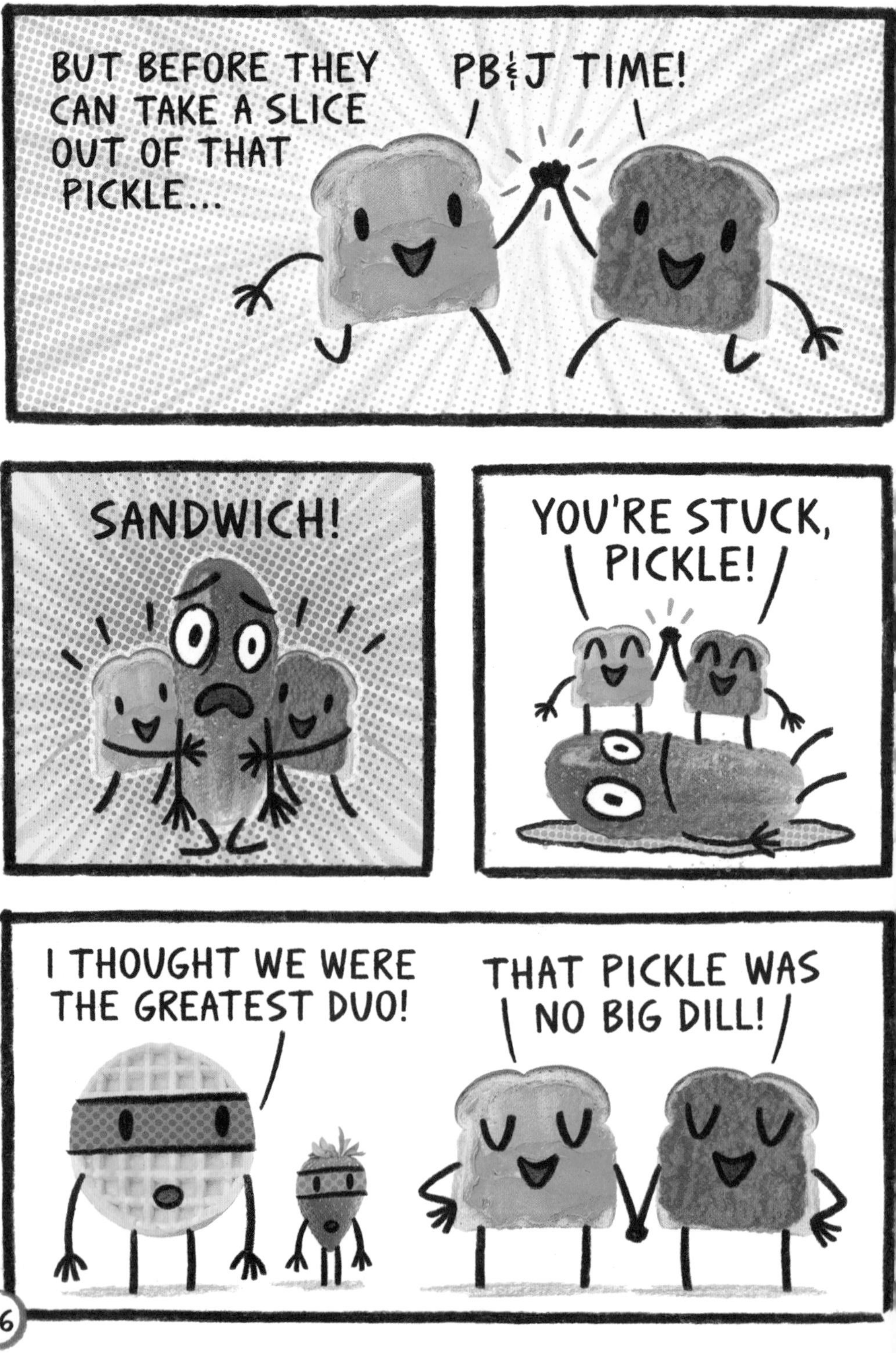
BUT BEFORE THEY CAN TAKE A SLICE OUT OF THAT PICKLE...
PB&J TIME!
SANDWICH!
YOU'RE STUCK, PICKLE!
I THOUGHT WE WERE THE GREATEST DUO!
THAT PICKLE WAS NO BIG DILL!

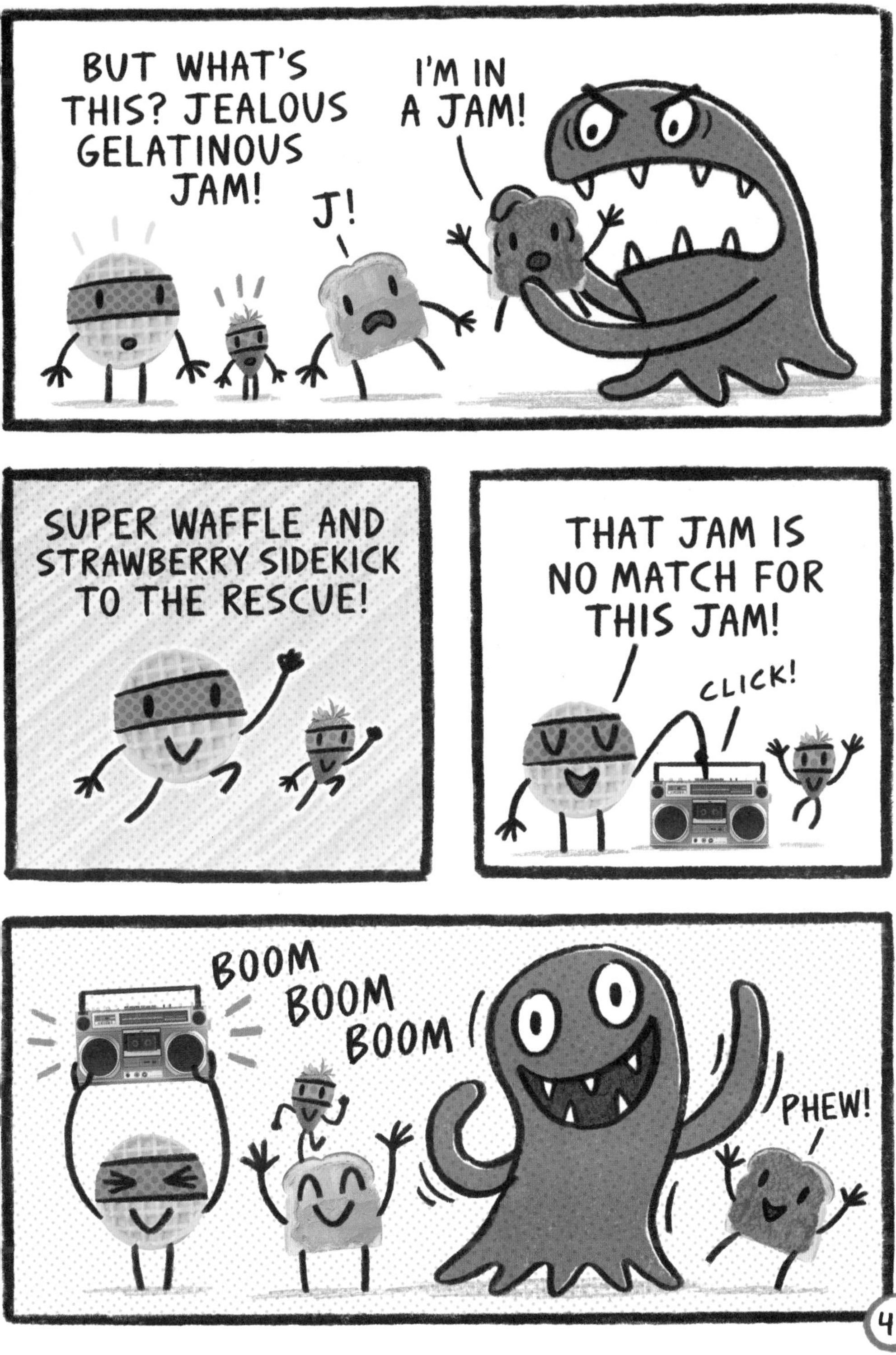
BUT WHAT'S THIS? JEALOUS GELATINOUS JAM!
I'M IN A JAM!
J!
SUPER WAFFLE AND STRAWBERRY SIDEKICK TO THE RESCUE!
THAT JAM IS NO MATCH FOR THIS JAM!
CLICK!
BOOM BOOM BOOM
PHEW!

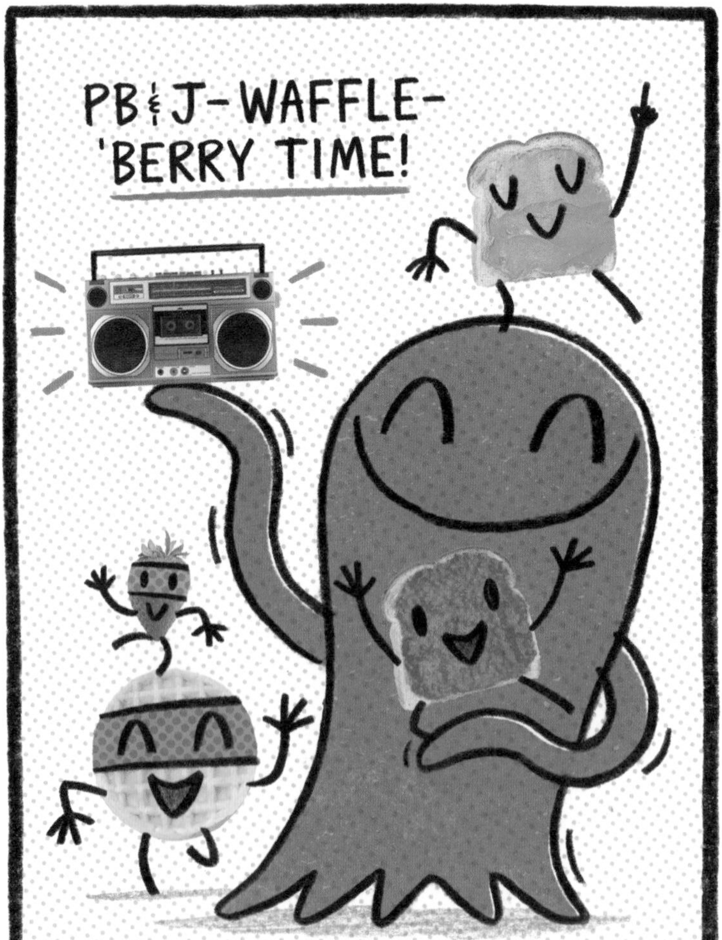
PB & J-WAFFLE-'BERRY TIME!

PEANUT

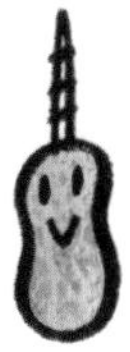

A.K.A. mini
NARWHAL

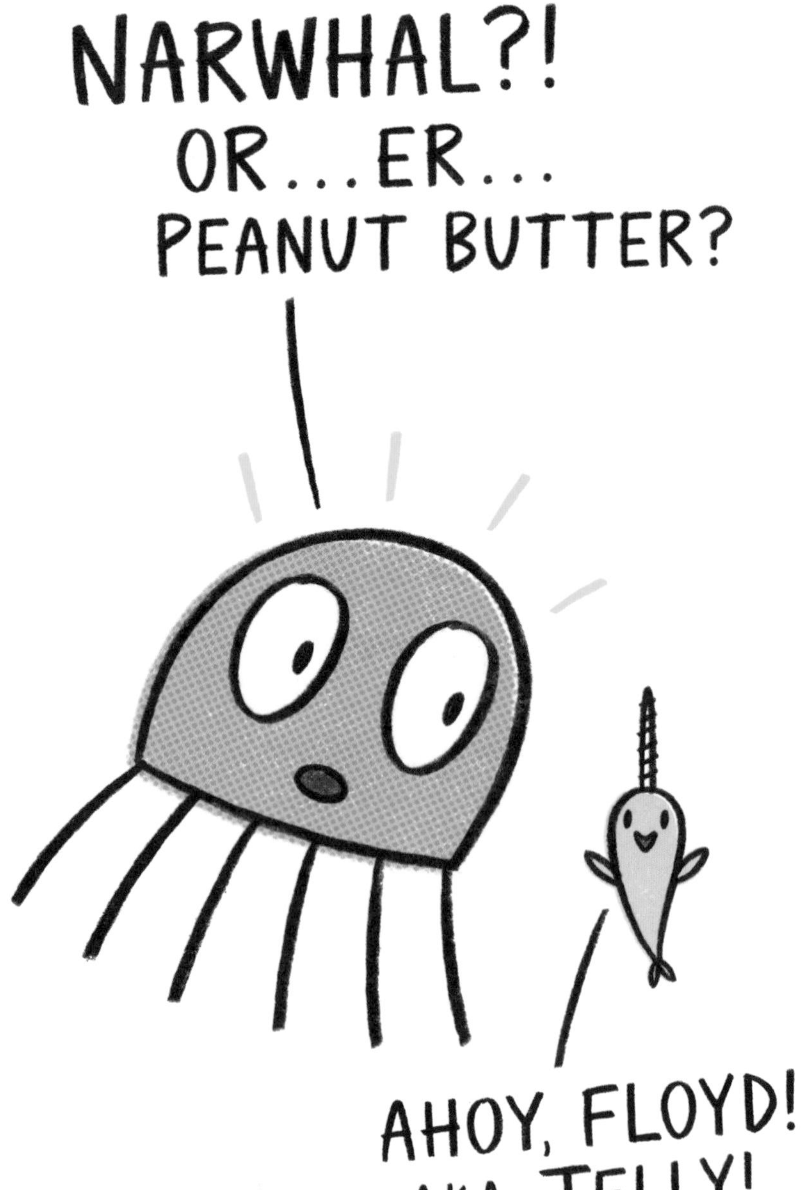
NARWHAL?!
OR...ER...
PEANUT BUTTER?
AHOY, FLOYD!
A.K.A. JELLY!

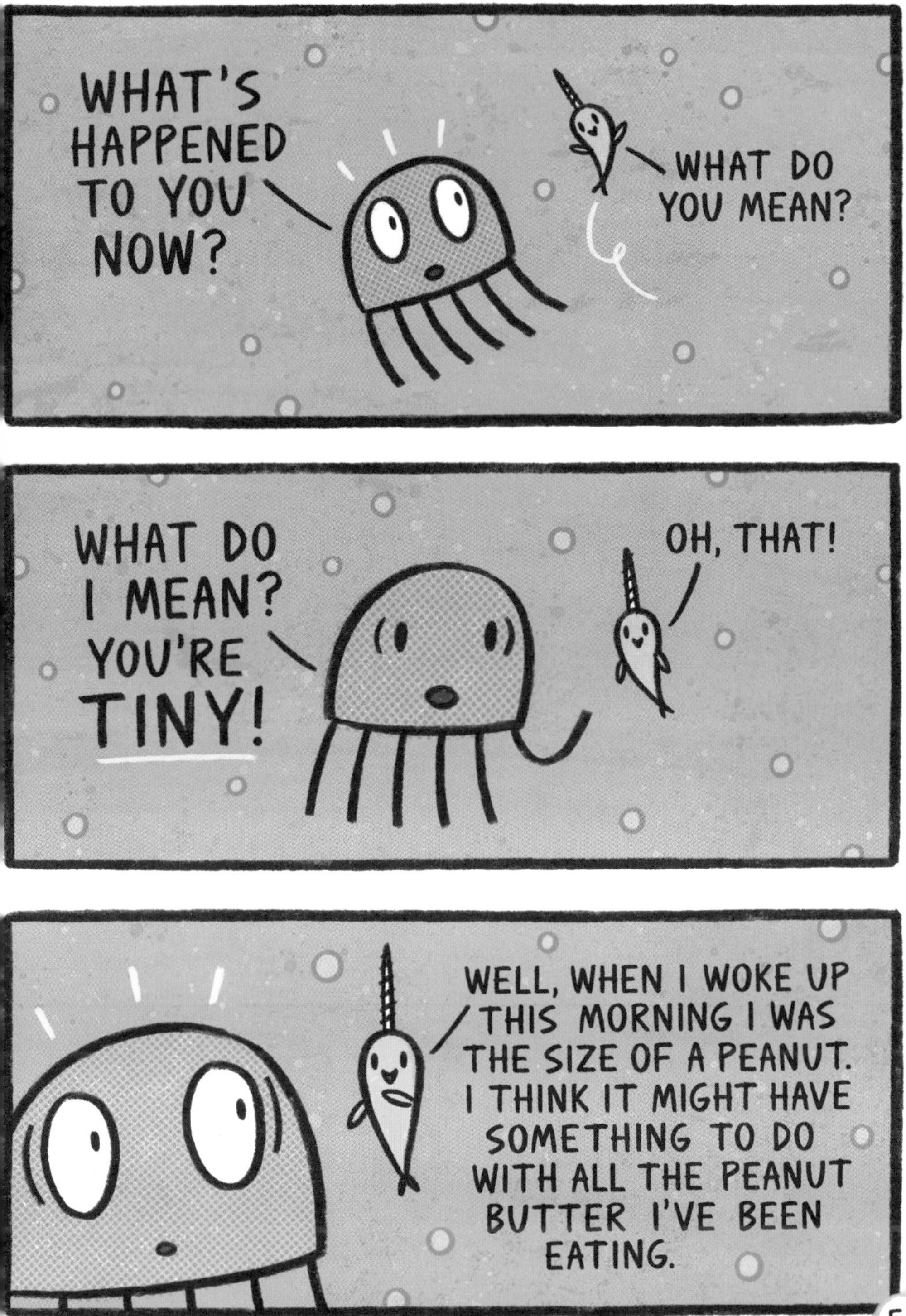
WHAT'S HAPPENED TO YOU NOW?
WHAT DO YOU MEAN?
WHAT DO I MEAN? YOU'RE TINY!
OH, THAT!
WELL, WHEN I WOKE UP THIS MORNING I WAS THE SIZE OF A PEANUT. I THINK IT MIGHT HAVE SOMETHING TO DO WITH ALL THE PEANUT BUTTER I'VE BEEN EATING.

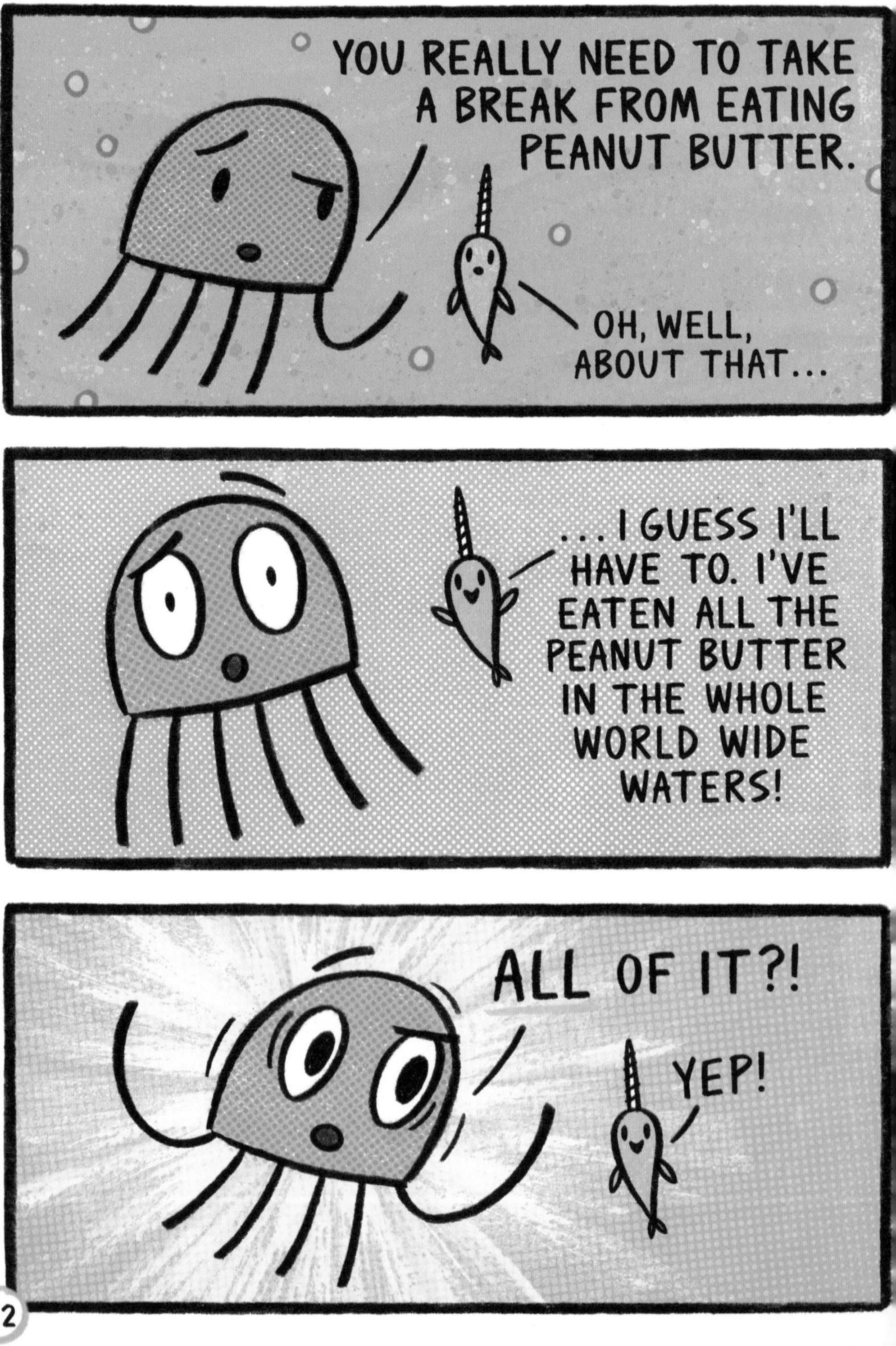
YOU REALLY NEED TO TAKE A BREAK FROM EATING PEANUT BUTTER.
OH, WELL, ABOUT THAT...
...I GUESS I'LL HAVE TO. I'VE EATEN ALL THE PEANUT BUTTER IN THE WHOLE WORLD WIDE WATERS!
ALL OF IT?!
YEP!

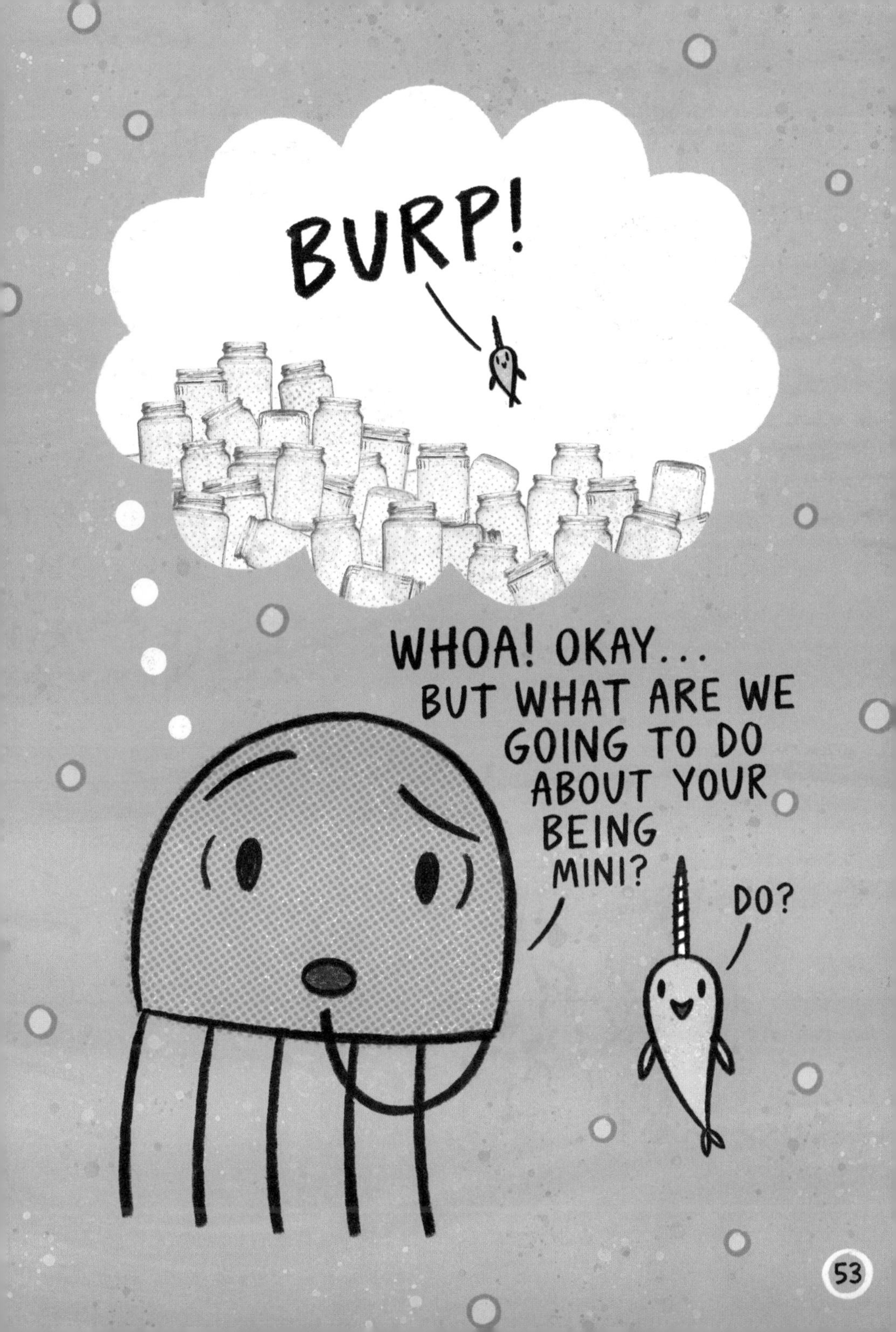
BURP!
WHOA! OKAY... BUT WHAT ARE WE GOING TO DO ABOUT YOUR BEING MINI?
DO?

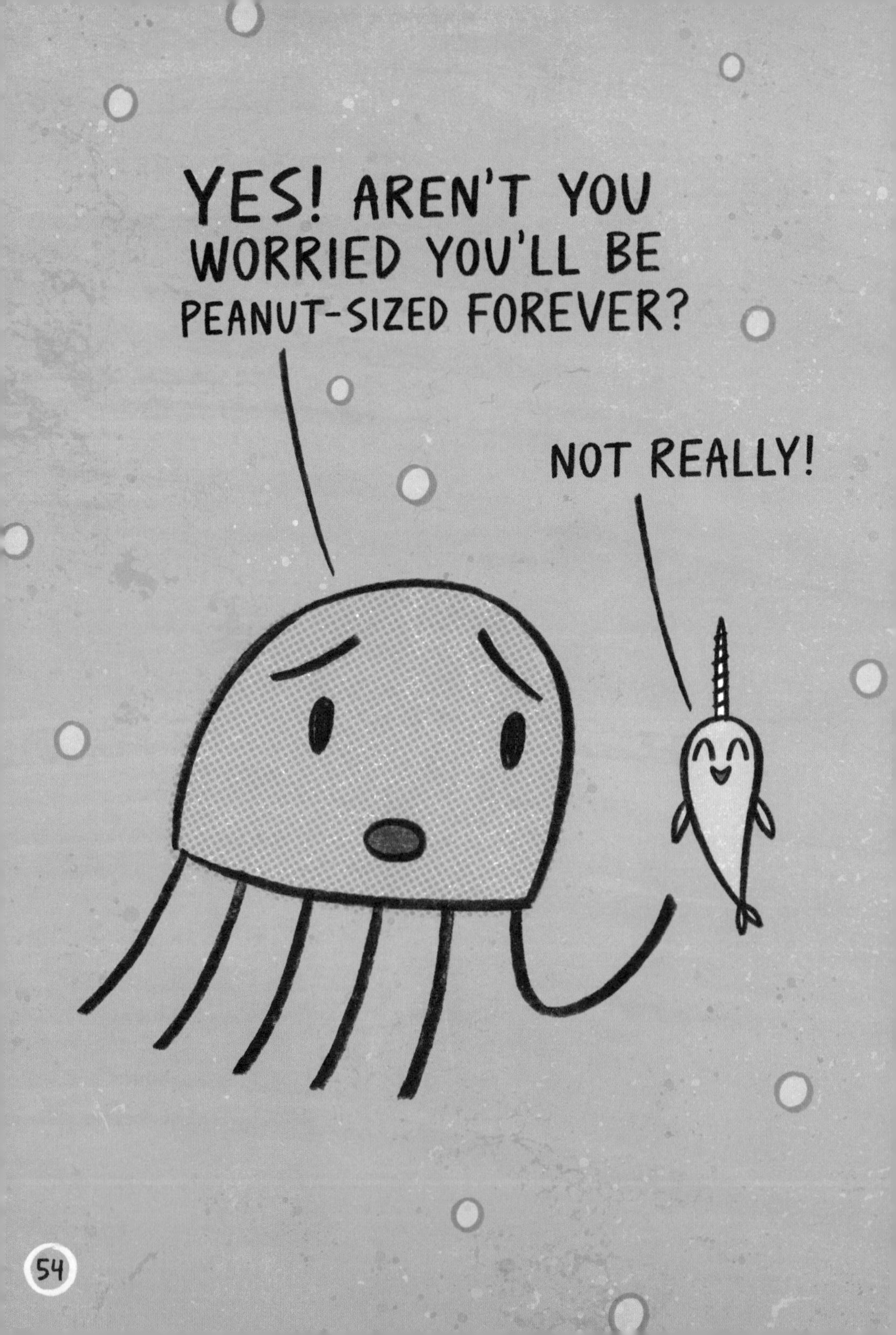
YES! AREN'T YOU WORRIED YOU'LL BE PEANUT-SIZED FOREVER?
NOT REALLY!

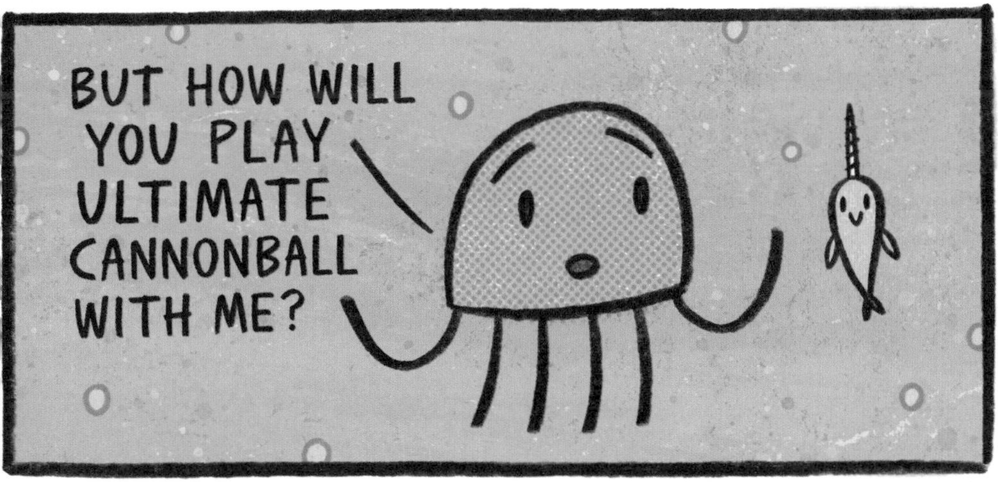
BUT HOW WILL YOU PLAY ULTIMATE CANNONBALL WITH ME?

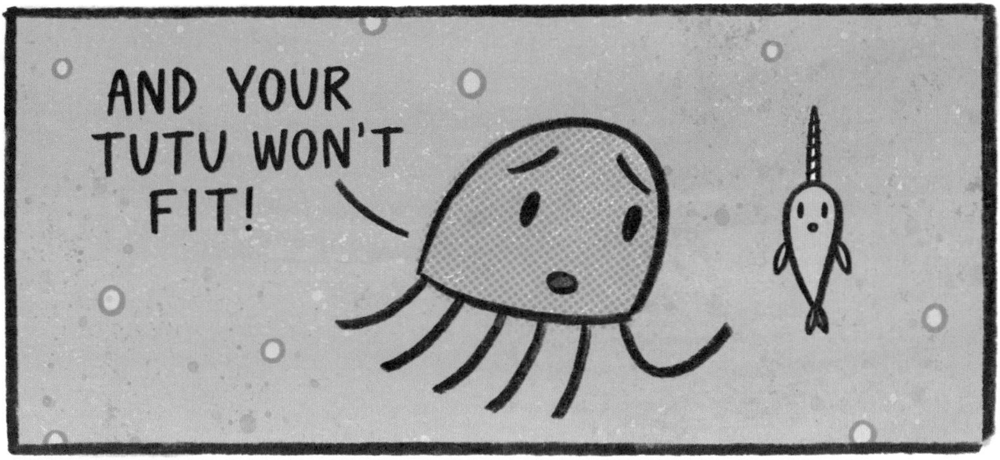
AND YOUR TUTU WON'T FIT!

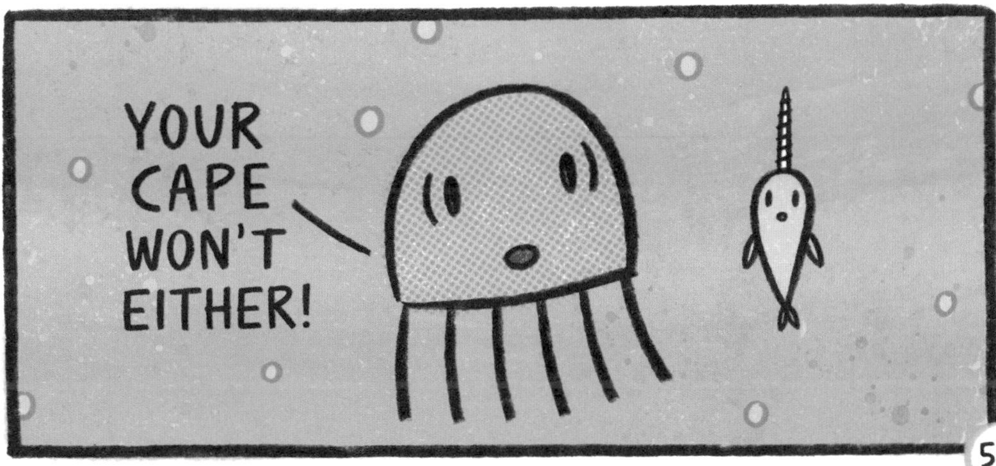
YOUR CAPE WON'T EITHER!

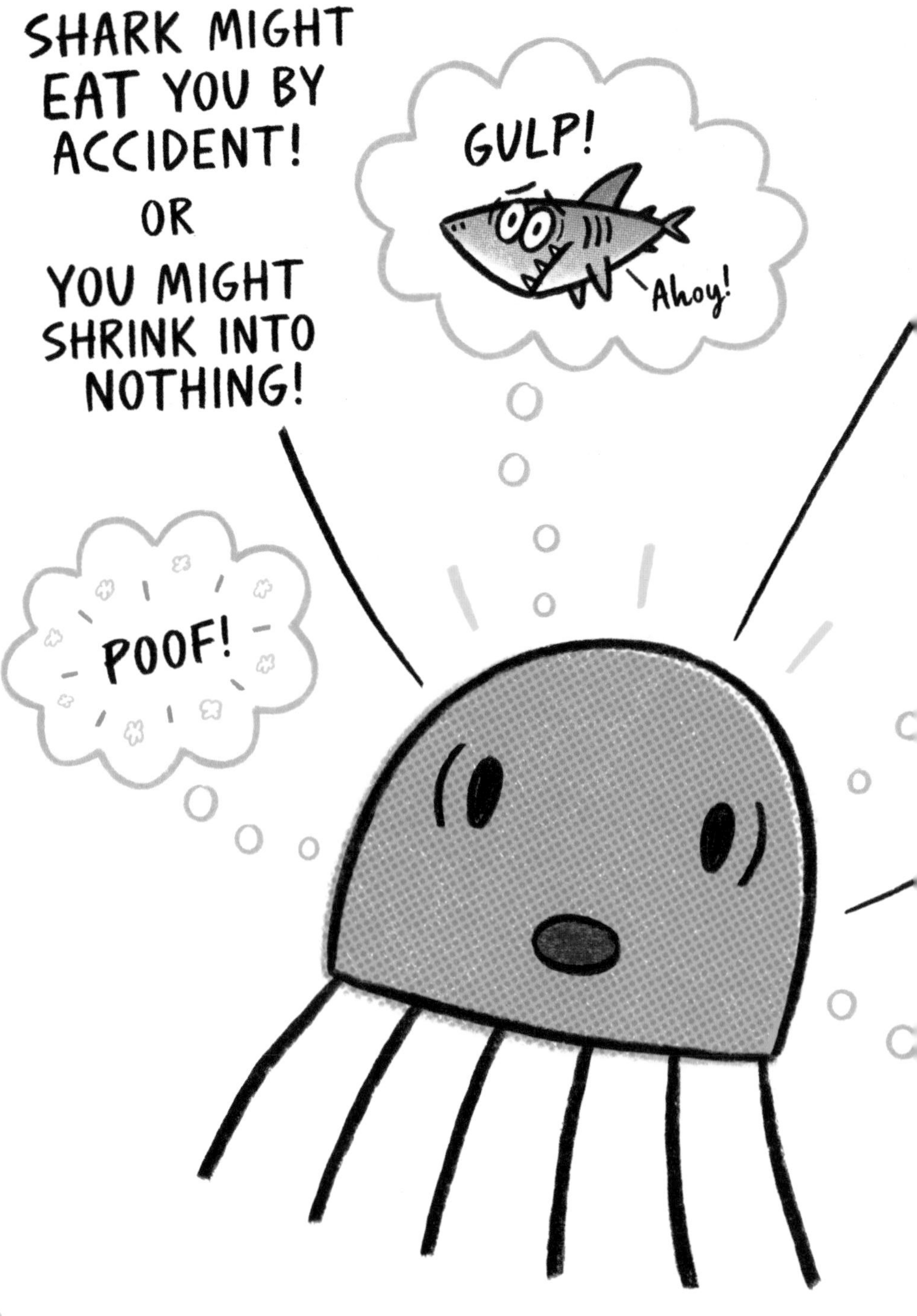
SHARK MIGHT EAT YOU BY ACCIDENT!
OR
YOU MIGHT SHRINK INTO NOTHING!
GULP!
Ahoy!
POOF!

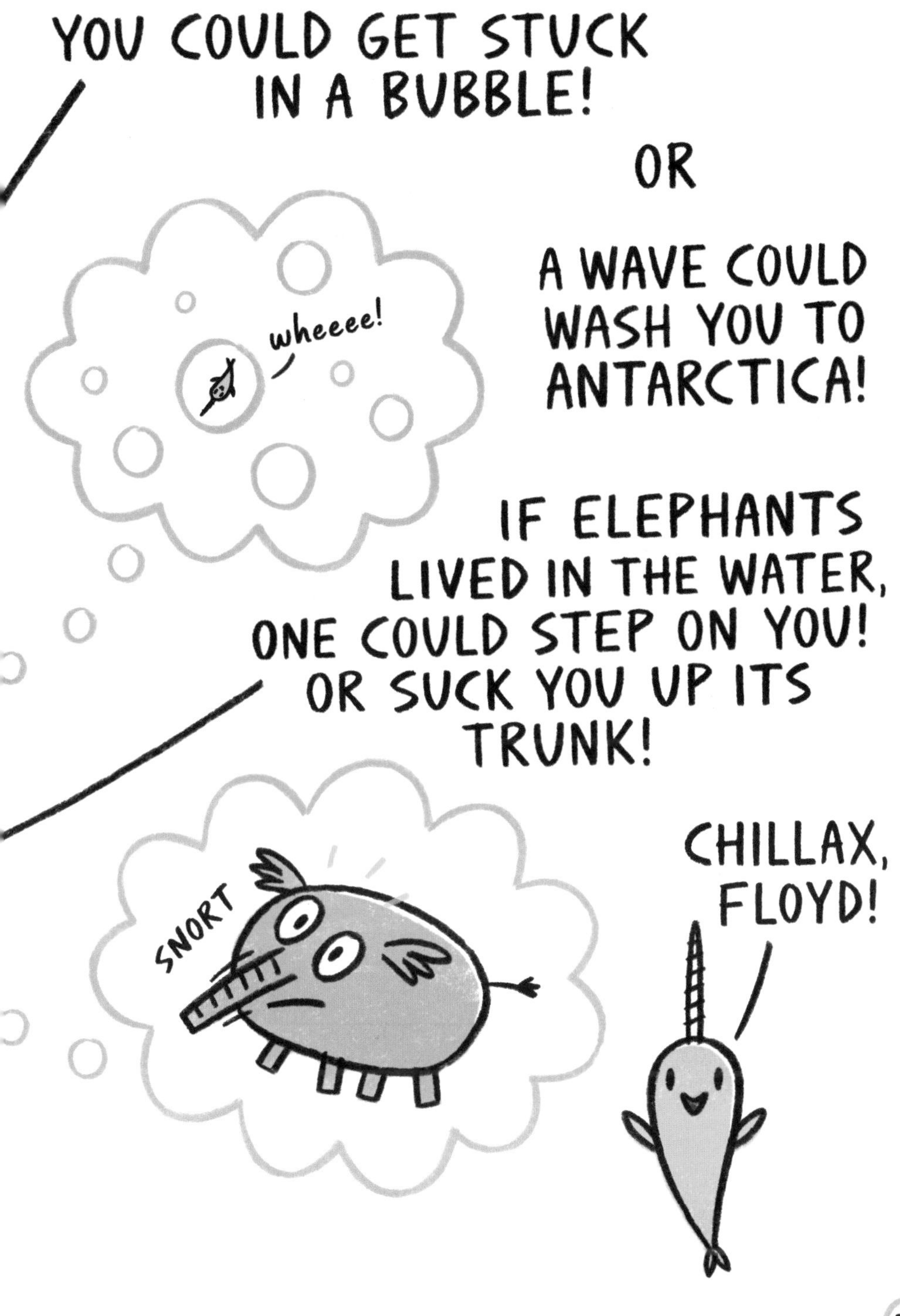
YOU COULD GET STUCK IN A BUBBLE!
wheeee!
OR
A WAVE COULD WASH YOU TO ANTARCTICA!
IF ELEPHANTS LIVED IN THE WATER, ONE COULD STEP ON YOU! OR SUCK YOU UP ITS TRUNK!
SNORT
CHILLAX, FLOYD!

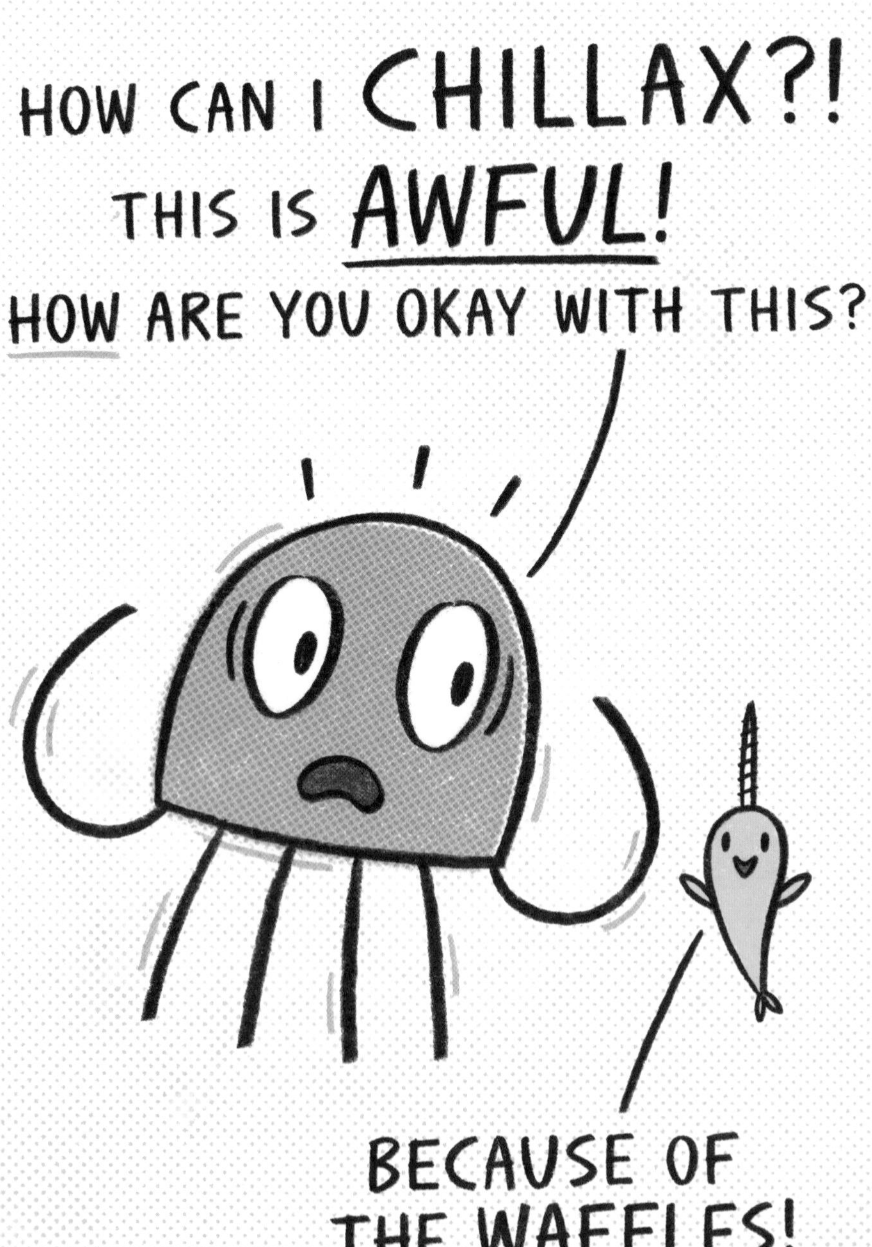
HOW CAN I CHILLAX?! THIS IS AWFUL! HOW ARE YOU OKAY WITH THIS?
BECAUSE OF THE WAFFLES!

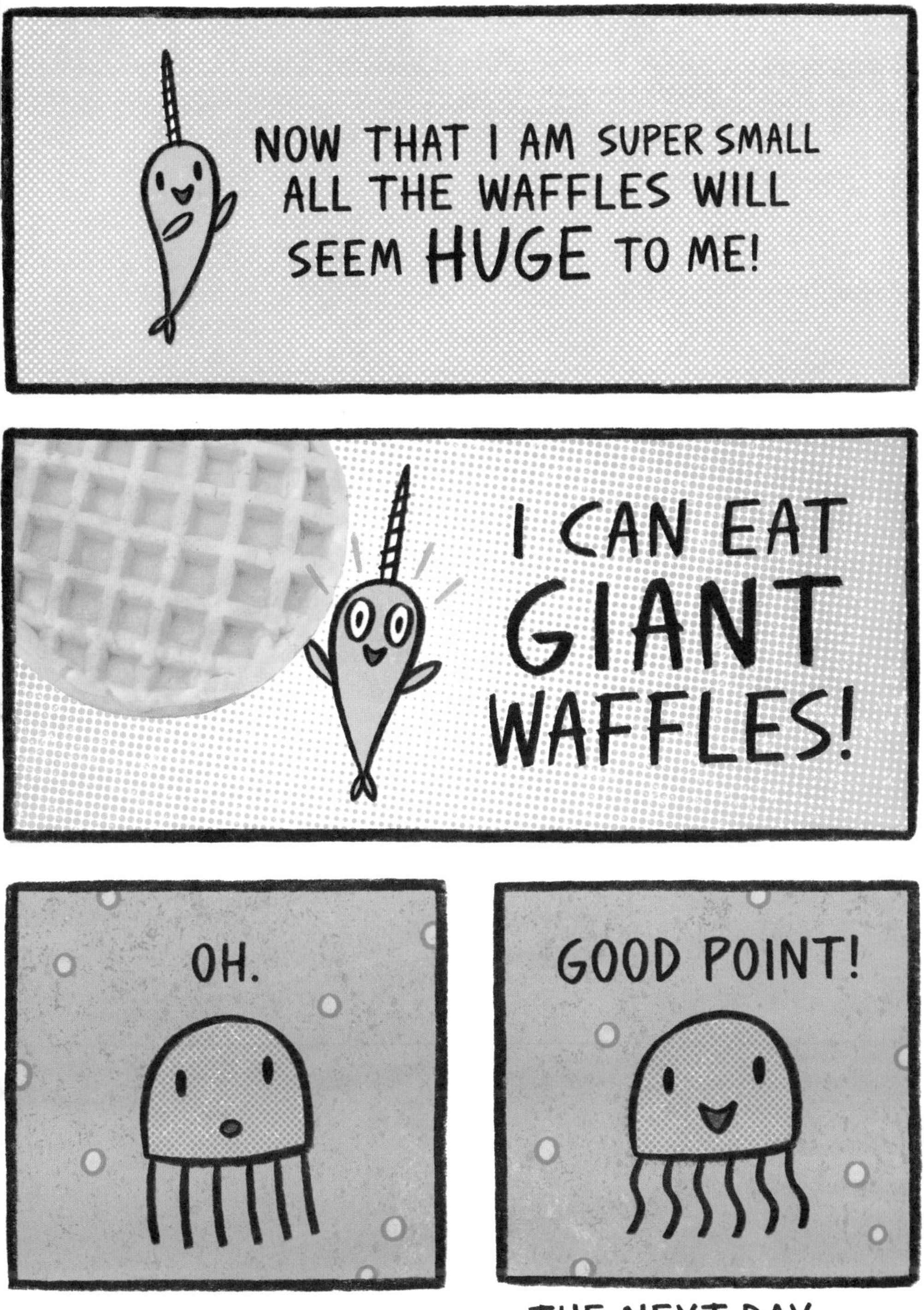
NOW THAT I AM SUPER SMALL ALL THE WAFFLES WILL SEEM HUGE TO ME!
I CAN EAT GIANT WAFFLES!
OH.
GOOD POINT!

THE NEXT DAY...

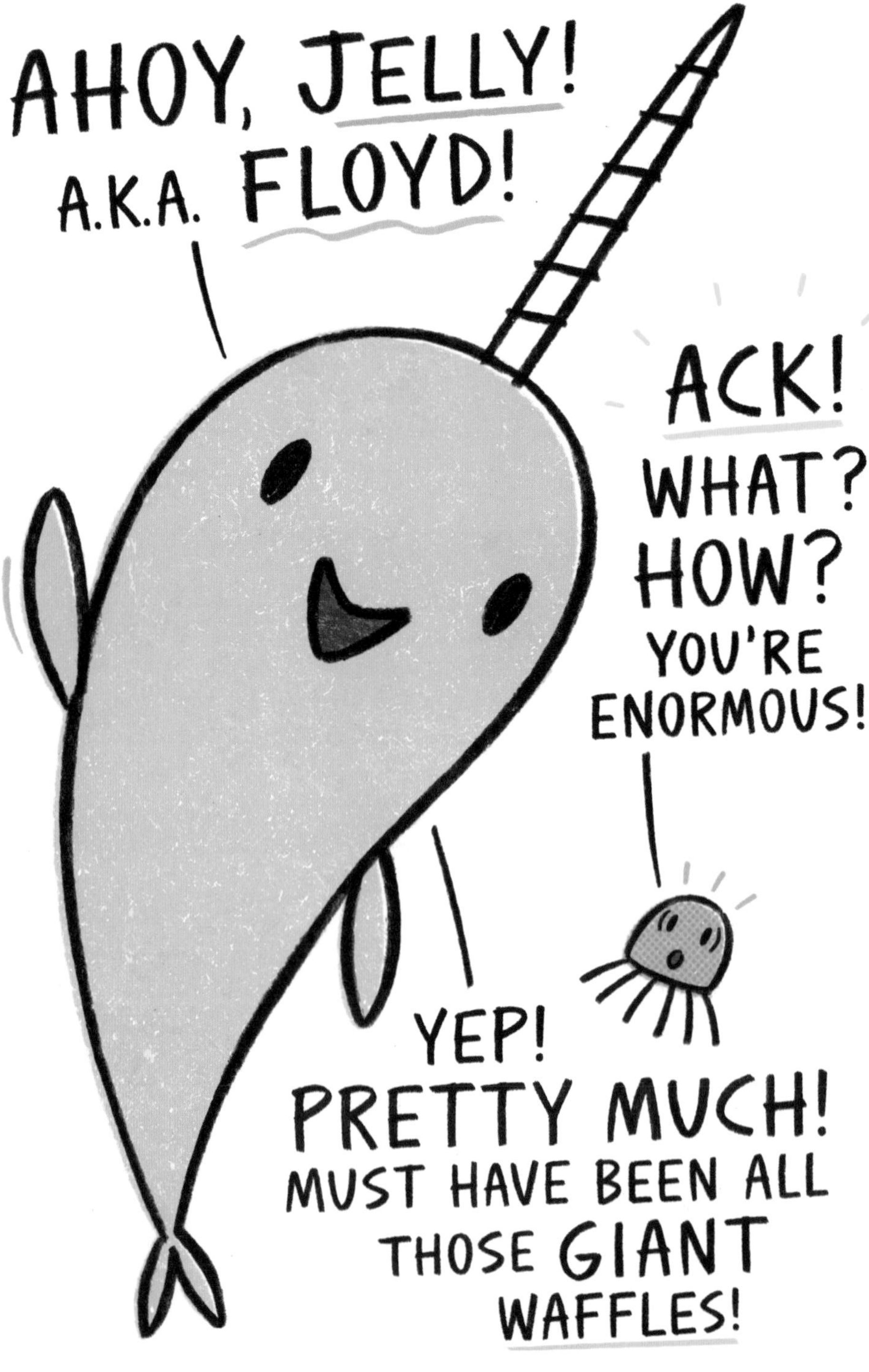
AHOY, JELLY! A.K.A. FLOYD!
ACK! WHAT? HOW? YOU'RE ENORMOUS!
YEP! PRETTY MUCH! MUST HAVE BEEN ALL THOSE GIANT WAFFLES!

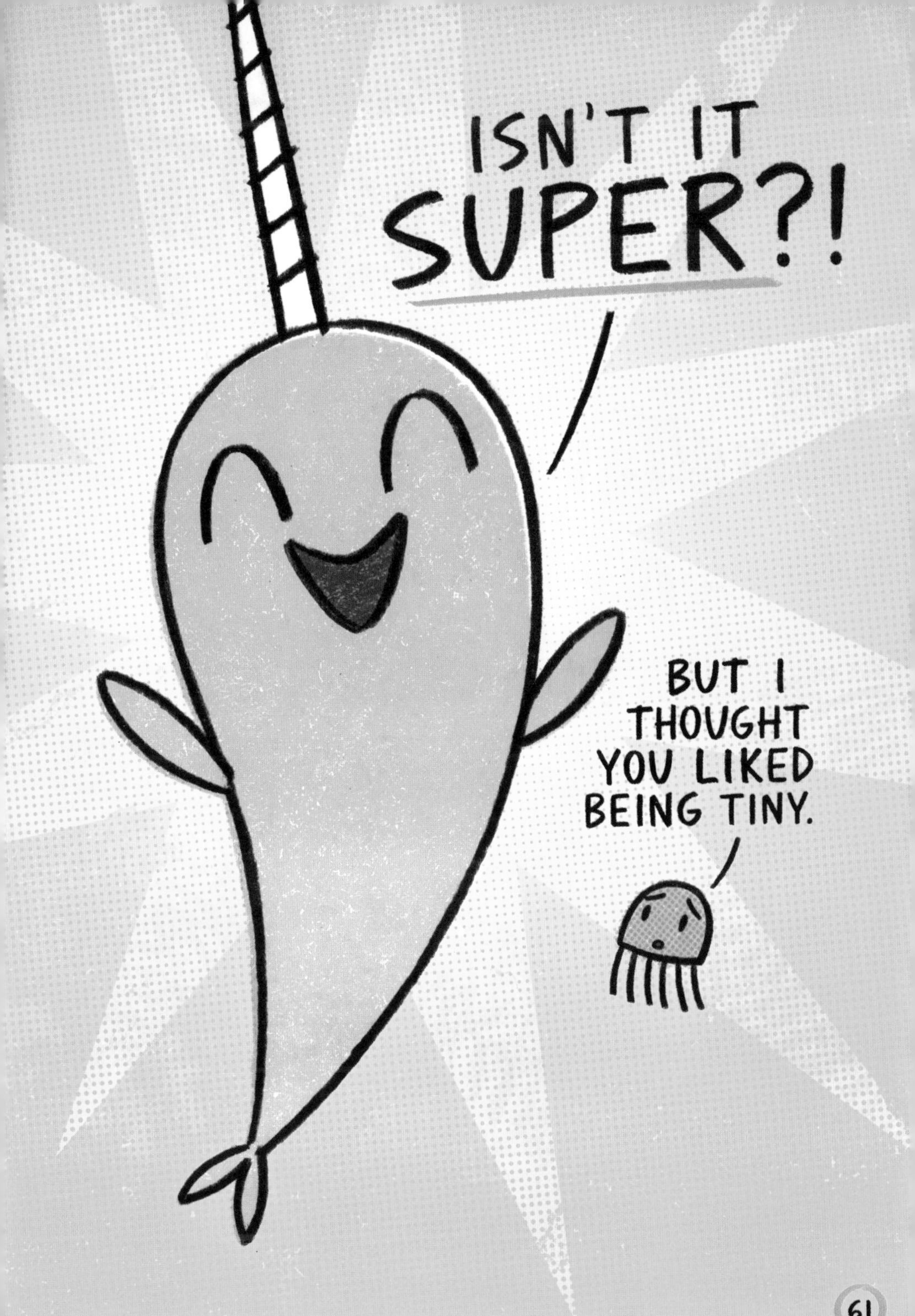
ISN'T IT SUPER?!
BUT I THOUGHT YOU LIKED BEING TINY.

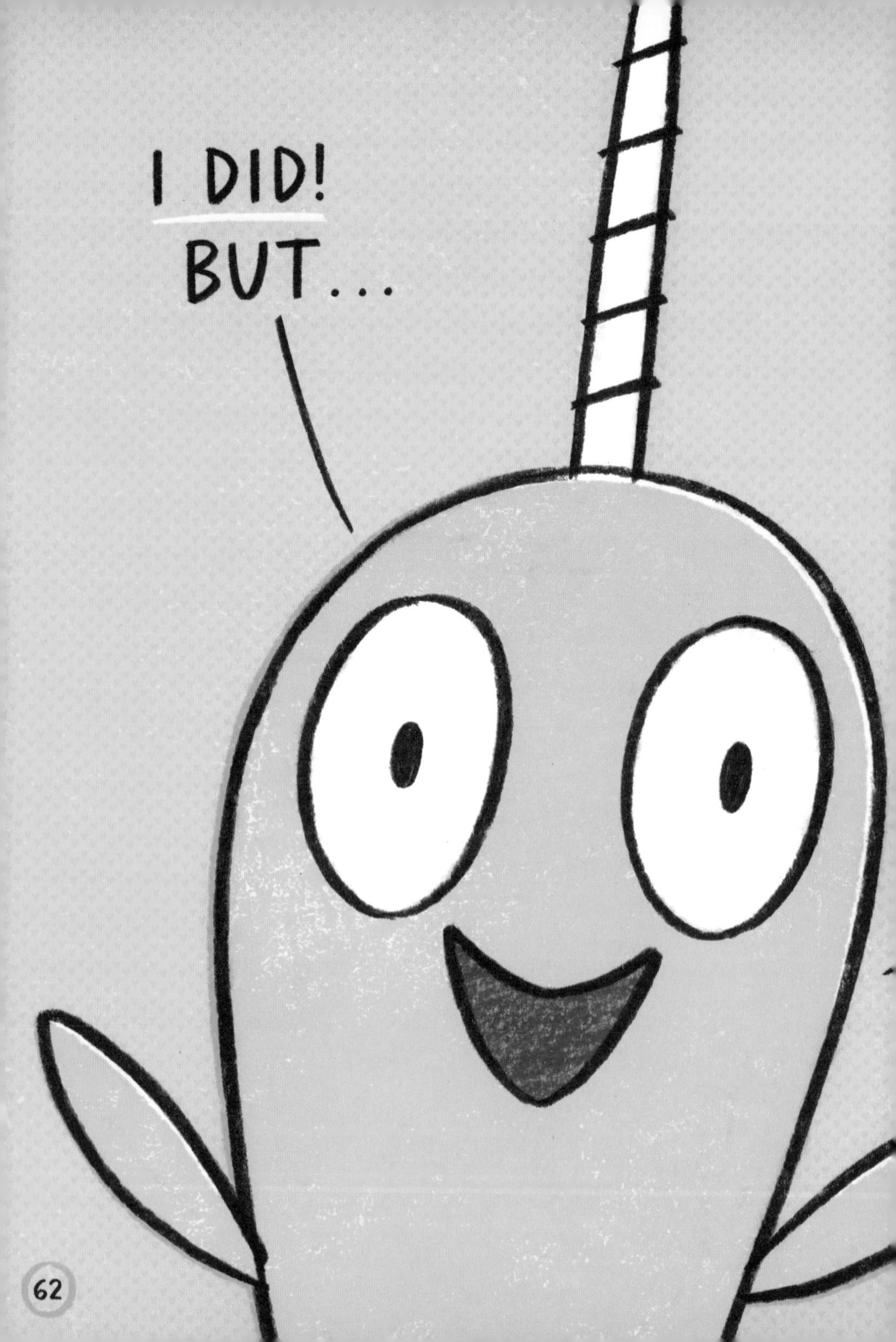
I DID! BUT...

... NOW THAT I'M **ENORMOUS** I CAN EAT OODLES OF WAFFLES! I'LL BREAK THE WORLD RECORD FOR WAFFLE EATING!

THAT IS... INGENIOUS!

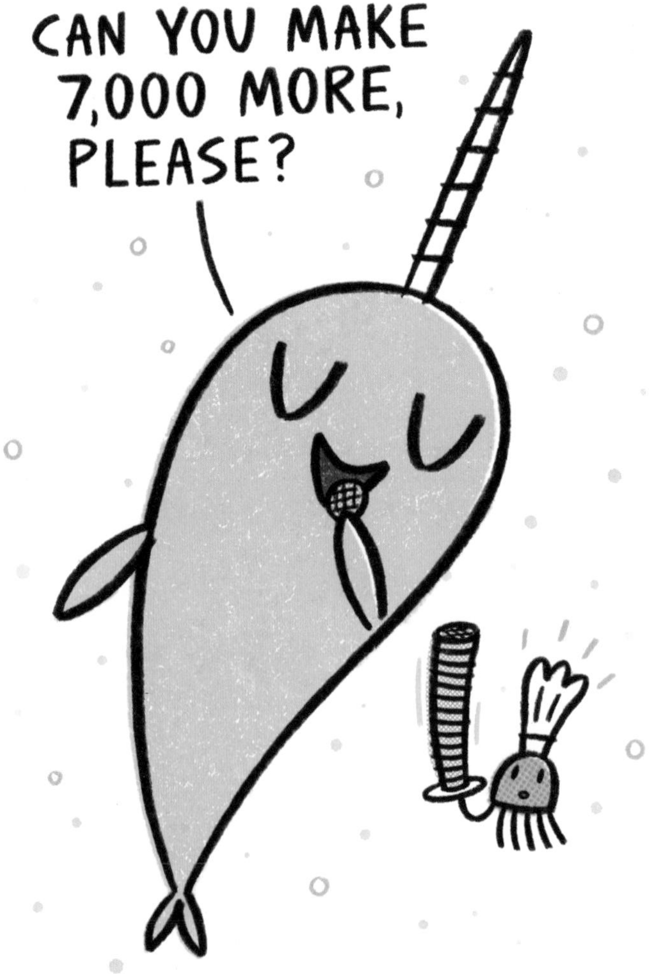
CAN YOU MAKE
7,000 MORE,
PLEASE?

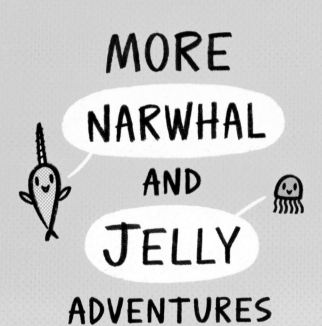

MORE
NARWHAL
AND
JELLY
ADVENTURES
COMING SOON!

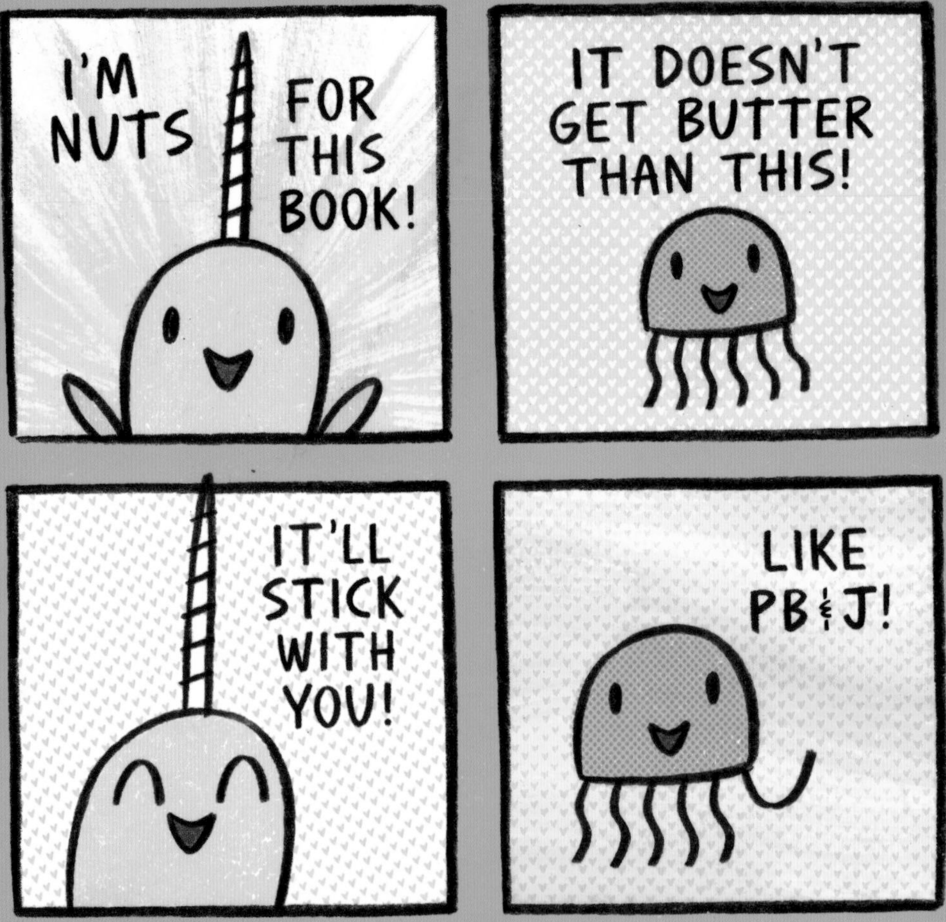
I'M NUTS FOR THIS BOOK!
IT DOESN'T GET BUTTER THAN THIS!
IT'LL STICK WITH YOU!
LIKE PB&J!

BEN CLANTON (A.K.A. CLANTOONS)

MAKES BOOKS! BOOKS LIKE MO'S MUSTACHE AND THE NARWHAL AND JELLY SERIES, INCLUDING EISNER AWARD-WINNER NARWHAL: UNICORN OF THE SEA! BEN ALSO EATS PB&J SANDWICHES. HE ATE 41 OF THEM WHILE MAKING THIS BOOK.

BENCLANTON.COM NARWHALANDJELLY.COM

tundra
www.penguinrandomhouse.ca

A JUNIOR LIBRARY GUILD SELECTION

House on Water,
House in Air

Fred Marchant

DEDALUS